To my own intrepid young explorers, Jessica and Dylan, who have made it all the way to Australia! Thanks also to my brave test pilots, Lara, Sean and Madz. Many thanks to Jill for letting me in the back way, and to Amy who taught me how to speak American properly.

PROLOGUE

In many ways, Fintan Fedora had been born very lucky. He had a friendly personality, a rich family, a nice house, and was the only boy at his school with a personal butler and an endless supply of cakes and biscuits. In other ways, however, Fintan was less lucky. He was a walking disaster area. He was appallingly clumsy and accident-prone. He also had a very poor sense of direction and, to be brutally honest, wasn't particularly bright. His father had once described him as having the brains of a damp sock – an old, worn out, damp sock at that. Fintan was nothing like his older brother and sister, who appeared to be good at everything they did. He'd just been born a bit different.

The kindest word to use when describing

Fintan's childhood would be "interesting". The kindest, perhaps, but probably not the most honest. "Disastrous" would be a better word. His nursery school had been forced to close down not long after he joined, when he somehow managed to fill it with wasps. No one ever worked out how Fintan had done this, but it had something to do with several jars of jam and a very large water pistol. Fintan had later been thrown out of two other schools after unfortunate incidents involving a flooded gymnasium and a few collapsed ceilings. At twelve, he had failed all his exams. Not because he hadn't studied, but because he never managed to find his way to the examination hall. At his last attempt he had ended up in the school kitchen and accidentally locked himself in a larder for the weekend.

If it hadn't been for Gribley, the family butler, looking after Fintan all these years, things might have turned out even worse. It had been Gribley who disposed of the unexploded bomb that Fintan found in a field and brought home to show his mother. It was Gribley who managed to get all the tigers back into their cage after that dreadful day out at the zoo. It was entirely thanks to Gribley saving him from many, many disasters that Fintan had survived to the age of fourteen at all.

In short, Fintan was a lot of work.

ONE

The heat was unbearable. The air was thick with a thousand irritating little insects, crawling in Fintan's ears and up his nose. Sweat trickled down his back and legs and soaked into his thick woolly jungle socks. Gasping for breath, Fintan slashed and hacked his way through the foliage, the spiky exotic plants scratching at his face.

"It's no good, I can't go on!" he wailed, leaning against a mossy tree trunk and wiping his brow. "We're never going to find it in all this undergrowth. It's hopeless!"

"I fear you may be right, sir," came the calm, sensible voice of Gribley. "Perhaps it would be simpler just to buy another cricket ball."

Fintan took off his wide-brimmed hat and fanned

himself with it.

"I suppose so, Gribley," he sighed, "but it does mean our game has come to a sudden end . . . and it was my turn to bat, too!"

He was just hauling himself out of the undergrowth and back on to the beautifully kept lawn when his mother caught sight of him from the drawing room window.

"Fintan!" she shouted, with a voice that could crack mirrors and frighten dogs at a hundred paces. "What on earth do you think you're doing in my shrubbery? Kindly stop trampling all over my rhododendrons with your silly great boots!"

Fintan made a miffed sort of face, thrust his hands into his trouser pockets and kicked idly at a small prickly branch which had attached itself to his sock.

"Your father wants a word with you, by the way," concluded his mother, closing the drawing room window and returning her attention to her cacti collection. His father wanted a word? This wasn't something that happened very often. In fact, apart from the odd grunted "good morning" from behind his newspaper at the breakfast table, his father rarely spoke to him at all! Fintan wondered what he might have done wrong. Surely demolishing a rhododendron bush or two with a cricket bat wasn't serious enough to deserve a severe talking-to? This didn't sound good.

Fintan's older sister, Felicity, and his older brother, Flavian, were lounging in deck chairs on the lawn. There was nothing they enjoyed more than making fun of their accident-prone little brother and this was a perfect opportunity to do so.

"Oh dear! Looks like the idiot boy's in trouble again!" mocked Felicity loudly. "I wonder what he's broken this time?"

Flavian snorted with laughter and spilled a little of his drink. "Been naughty again, has he? Made his daddy cross?"

The pair of them laughed so hard at this thought that they had to wipe tears from their eyes and lemonade came out of their noses. Fintan ignored them as best he could. He'd been trying to ignore them for years.

Gribley coughed politely. "Perhaps you should go and see what your father wants, sir," he suggested. "And it would be wise to wash your face and hands first. I will see to it that the cricket equipment is cleared away."

After a quick splash in the wash basin, a slightly less grass-stained Fintan knocked on his father's study door.

"Come in," called a stern voice from within. Fintan pulled hard on the door handle, but it failed to open. He gave it a good hard tug, followed by a series of short rattling tugs, none of which achieved anything apart from making a lot of annoying noise.

"Push, you idiot!" said his father, sounding exasperated already. Fintan pushed with unnecessary force. He stumbled into the room like a drunk on roller skates, tripped over the rug and fell head first into a bookcase.

"Sorry, Dad!" he said, struggling to his feet and picking up some of the books from the floor. "I can never remember whether it's 'push' or 'pull' and—"

"Yes, yes, yes," interrupted his father, who had heard enough already. "Sit down, boy, I need to talk to you."

Fintan's father, Sir Filbert Fedora, was a formidable character. He was a large, old-fashioned-looking man with a ruddy face and a grey moustache the size of a fat squirrel. He had made his fortune in cakes. To be precise, he was the founder and chief executive of The Fedora Fancy Food Company – Purveyors of Fine Cakes and Biscuits. A huge portrait of him proudly holding a grand lemon tart assortment hung on the mahogany panelled wall behind him. Fintan sat in the squeaky red leather chair he was offered and peered nervously at his father across the enormous desk. Sir Filbert coughed into his hand, preparing to say something a little awkward.

"As you know, I'm not as young as I used to be..."

"Well, obviously you're not, Father! No one gets younger, do they! That would be impossi—"

"Will you please not interrupt me!" snapped his father. "Just listen! I'm getting to the age now where I'm considering retirement. Running The Fedora Fancy Food Company is too much work at my age, which is why I need to have this little chat with you..."

Fintan's eyebrows leapt up. He knew where this was leading. "No need to worry, Father!" he announced confidently. "The business will be safe in my hands. You can trust me!"

Sir Filbert coughed again, stood up and began

to pace around the room with his hands clasped behind his back.

"I'm afraid you misunderstand me, Fintan . . . the problem is that we can't trust you."

Fintan's face fell and was replaced with a look similar to that of a small puppy who had just been told off for weeing on the carpet.

"I'm sorry, son, it's just that your mother and I have been talking and we think once you finish school, your talents would be better suited to . . . er . . . well . . . to other areas. Leisure interests, for instance. I'm sure your brother and sister can manage the business perfectly well without you."

This last bit of news came as no surprise to Fintan. His goody-goody siblings, Felicity and Flavian, could do no wrong! They'd always been more popular, more successful and, well . . . more everything! This was terrible! It wasn't fair! It was unjust!

"But you *can* trust me!" he protested. "I'd be really good at running the business!"

His father stopped pacing and looked sternly at him. "Really?" he said, staring straight into Fintan's puppy-dog eyes. "We can trust you, can we? What about the time we got you that hamster?"

"That wasn't my fault!" pleaded Fintan. "It got in the vacuum cleaner all on its own!"

"Maybe so, but you didn't have to try and get it out by turning the machine to blow! The mess took nearly a week to clean up! And what about the time we trusted you to organize that barbecue? Your mother was furious when those three fire engines turned up! They ruined the lawn!"

Fintan pulled a hurt face. "That wasn't my fault either! How was I to know that red bucket had petrol in it?"

Sir Filbert raised a hand, as if to say there was no point in arguing about it. "That's enough!" he said. "I'm afraid I've made my decision. Sorry, son. You'll just have to find something else to do with your future."

Fintan returned to his room, sat miserably on his bed and fumed. He'd show his father he wasn't useless!

TWO

Meanwhile, approximately forty miles south of Fedora Hall, and to the left a bit, Mrs Edith Bumstead was cooking tea for her horrible spotty overweight son, Eric. Ignoring the cigarette ash she was dropping into her saucepan of baked beans, she scraped the burnt and blackened contents out on to a slice of stale white bread.

"Beans on bread?" said Eric, indignantly. "Couldn't we at least have toast? This is just bread! It's like . . . er . . . raw toast!"

His mother flicked her stinky brown cigarette into the huge pile of washing-up and wiped her hands on her cardigan. "It's not my fault the toaster's conked out. It hasn't worked properly since you put that beefburger in it!" she yelled.

Eric ignored this and pulled a stupid face, which was quite easy with a face like his. "But I'm fed up to the back teeth with beans, Mum! Why can't we have some proper food?"

Mrs Bumstead sat at the table next to her son and adopted a sad voice and a matching face. "Because we don't have much money, Eric. Things have been difficult since your dear father passed away, God rest his soul. . ."

"He didn't pass away, Mum!" shouted Eric. "He's in prison! I've known that for years, so you can stop pretending!"

"Anyway, you're fat enough as it is!" hollered Mrs Bumstead, changing the subject as quickly as she could. "You spend all your time lying about on the sofa watching the telly. If you could be bothered to go out and get a job, maybe we could afford something a bit more interesting to eat!"

Eric had recently left school with no qualifications, no prospects and no friends. The only thing he had to show for all his years in education was a large box of chalk stolen from the stationery cupboard and several catering-sized tins of beans stolen from the school kitchen. Since then, he hadn't worked a single day. His mother thrust the newspaper in his face, open at the job advertisements. Eric's attention, however, was drawn to a large picture on the opposite page. Beneath the headline *MILLIONAIRE CAKE TYCOON TO RETIRE* was a full-colour photograph of Sir Filbert Fedora and a long article on his life and successful business empire. It was the word "millionaire" that had attracted Eric's attention. Eagerly, he traced a finger through the paragraphs beneath, mumbling the words out loud as he did so. It appeared the Fedora family was one of the richest in England! It also appeared there was a fourteen-year-old son, who was the perfect target for kidnapping!

A big grin spread across Eric's fat, bean-juice-spattered face. "I've just had a brilliant idea!" he announced.

THREE

"I've just had a brilliant idea!' shouted Fintan, emerging from behind a copy of *Young Adventurer* magazine. "I know how to impress Father, and make millions of pounds for Fedora Fancies at the same time!"

"Really, sir? And how, may I ask, might you achieve such a thing?"

"With the great Brazilian chocoplum! That's how, Gribley!"

Gribley raised his eyebrows. Fintan thought he'd better explain.

"It's the rarest fruit in the entire world, Gribley. And according to the lucky few who have ever tasted one, it's the most delicious too!"

"But surely, sir, there's no such thing as the great

Brazilian chocoplum. I pride myself on having a wide knowledge of the world's exotic foodstuffs, and I'm afraid I've never heard of it."

Fintan smiled and waved his magazine. "Ah, yes, well, some say it's just a myth! A story passed down by generations of Amazon Indians. But not according to this article in *Young Adventurer* magazine. Look, there are reports of a small group of great Brazilian chocoplum trees being discovered deep in the rainforest!"

Gribley still didn't look convinced. In fact, he looked extremely unconvinced. This sounded like yet another one of Fintan's silly ideas, and over the fourteen years he had been employed in the Fedora household, there had been rather a lot of them. Gribley was reminded of the time Fintan had read that article on "the science of alchemy" and the week they had spent in the garden shed attempting to make gold out of cat food and washing-up liquid. The experiments had only been abandoned when several hungry cats invaded the shed, attacked them both and ate the test materials. It had taken a further week to clean up the mess, as cats aren't very good at digesting washing-up liquid. Gribley wished Fintan wouldn't read these types of magazines! They tended to fill his head full of dangerous ideas and adventurous nonsense.

"Any idea where Brazil is, Gribley?" asked Fintan, excitedly spinning his illuminated globe. "Is it anywhere near France?"

Twenty minutes later, armed with his *Big Boy's Atlas of the World*, his diary and the Brazilian chocoplum article carefully bookmarked in his *Young Adventurer* magazine, Fintan proudly presented his expedition idea to his parents. There was a moment's shocked silence after he finished speaking. His mother, who had no idea what to say, looked pleadingly at his father.

"A splendid idea!" announced Sir Filbert eventually, much to everyone's surprise. Fintan could hardly believe his ears. "Really?" he said. "Do you mean that?"

"Certainly, my boy," lied his father, through a big false grin. "A bit of adventure! Splendid! I'm sure it will do you a power of good!" He didn't actually mean this for a second, of course. In fact, he was pretty sure Fintan would find it difficult to get out of Fedora Hall without getting lost or forgetting where he was going, let alone make it to Brazil! What he actually thought was that this was a far better idea than letting Fintan anywhere near the family business. If he was off wandering around on the other side of the world, he would be out of harm's way. He could be someone else's problem for a while.

"Gribley will have to accompany you, of course," he added.

"Brilliant!" shouted Fintan. "I'll go and start planning the expedition right away!"

For some reason, Gribley didn't look quite so excited by this turn of events. In fact, he looked completely stunned. Having to accompany young Fintan, the walking disaster area, on a foolish trip to the Amazon rainforest wasn't his idea of fun at all! It didn't bear thinking about.

Fintan could barely contain his excitement. A real expedition! Proper explorer stuff! Just what he'd always dreamed of! "I reckon the trip should take us about a month, Gribs," he declared, already scribbling his ideas down on a piece of paper. "So we're going to need to pack quite a lot of provisions.

Any idea how many peanut butter sandwiches we'll need to last a month?"

Gribley closed his eyes and let out a slight whimper.

FOUR

Fintan and Gribley weren't the only ones making travel plans. Eric and Edith Bumstead were at that very moment studying a tatty old map of England, trying to locate the little village where Fedora Hall stood. It didn't help that neither of them were particularly good at reading and that Mrs Bumstead couldn't see much without her glasses.

"There it is, look!" shouted Eric, triumphantly stabbing his finger at a small black square in the middle of the North Sea. "No, wait . . . that's an oil rig . . . can't be that, then."

"Remind me," said his mother, who was having trouble keeping up. "What are we supposed to be doing again?"

Eric rolled his eyes impatiently. "I've told you

twice already, Mum! We're going to kidnap that Fedora boy and demand a ransom from his rich parents! It's simple! We just need to find where they live."

"Kidnap him, eh?" said Edith, rubbing her chin and suddenly sounding very interested. "And they're really rich, are they? How much do you think we could get for him in ransom money?"

"At least a million quid, I reckon!" announced Eric proudly. "His dad's a millionaire! He can afford to pay up!"

In his head, Eric was already a very successful kidnapper – and a very rich, successful kidnapper at that. There would be no more eating burnt beans on stale bread for him! A future of unimaginable riches and luxury was opening up: gold-plated bath taps in the shape of swans! In fact, why not a gold-plated bath in the shape of a swan? He could afford anything! A big posh house, a shiny red sports car or two parked outside, caviar and chips for tea every night! This plan was the best idea he'd ever had, though to be honest, he hadn't had many so it wasn't saying much. He was going to be stinking rich, though; that was what mattered. . .

"I'm going to be stinking rich!" he said, grinning broadly.

"Don't you mean WE are going to be stinking rich?" countered his mother.

Eric made a sort of grunting noise, which was meant to sound as if he was agreeing, but without actually doing so.

"Just concentrate on the plan, will you," he said. "I might need you to help as a look-out or something."

FIVE

A few days later, after a bit of a struggle and a lot of shoving from below, Edith Bumstead had managed to clamber up a tree just outside the grounds of Fedora Hall and was surveying the house through a pair of binoculars.

"I can see him!" she hissed to her son on her stolen mobile phone. "He's in that upstairs room there! The third window from the left."

Eric had dragged his fat little body over the wall and was crawling commando-style across the Fedoras' lawn towards a large bush which had been clipped into the shape of a peacock.

"Message received and understood!" he hissed back, feeling very important. "Any idea how I'm going to get up there?" he added, hoping there wasn't a drainpipe he'd have to climb up. He was exhausted enough after scaling the garden wall.

"Hang on a minute," said his mother, scanning the scene, "Yeah! Over by the greenhouse, there's something that looks like a ladder! I think it's a ladder."

This was encouraging news to Eric, who was now hiding behind the big peacock-shaped bush. "OK! Let me know when the coast's clear and I'll make a dash for it!"

It wasn't so much a dash as an unfit waddle, but Eric did eventually make it across the rest of the lawn to the cover of the greenhouse. "Right!" he hissed down the phone line. "This is it! I'm going in!" He dragged the ladder to the house as stealthily as possible and quietly leaned it up against Fintan's window.

Inside Fedora Hall, preparations for the great Brazilian trip were almost complete. "Are you sure you have your passport, Master Fintan?" asked Gribley for the third time.

"Quite sure, thanks!" said Fintan proudly. "It's right here on my dressing table, ready to go! How about yourself? All packed?"

"Indeed, sir. I have just double-checked the list. We have all our camping equipment, clothing, boots, cooking utensils, first-aid kits, medicines, mosquito nets, repair kits, maps, compass, travel documents, foreign currency and air tickets. You need only be sure you have your own personal items and passport, sir. Now, if you'll excuse me, I'll begin carrying our things to the car."

Fintan was thoroughly excited. This was even better than the school coach trip he had taken to the Welsh mountains. And with any luck would be less of a disaster, too. He still denied rolling the coach's spare wheel down a mountain, and anyway it wasn't so much the lost wheel that had annoyed the mountain rescue team, but the seven hours they had spent looking for Fintan, who went to get it back. Luckily this time they weren't going in a coach and Fintan had been banned from "helping" with anything mechanical.

"Do you think I should leave a window open while we're away?" called Fintan from his bedroom. "To keep the room aired?"

"I don't think that will be necessary, sir," replied Gribley, who was busy hauling a heavy rucksack down the stairs.

"I suppose you're right, Gribley. It's a bit chilly, actually."

Having just flung his bedroom window wide open and immediately shut it again, Fintan managed to miss two quite interesting things. First, he failed to see the horrified expression on the face of the little fat man clinging to a ladder as it was tipped over backwards. Secondly, he didn't hear the terrifying crashing of glass as the man disappeared through the roof of his mum's greenhouse and into her cacti collection. He did hear a few muffled howls of pain but thought he must be imagining it.

"Right, then! We're all set!" he said happily, rubbing his hands together with anticipation. "Let's hit the road!"

A few minutes of farewells followed, during which Fintan's father shook his hand manfully and his mother fussed and made sure he'd packed plenty of vests. Felicity and Flavian strolled over to offer a few last-minute sarcastic comments.

"Look at that!" sniggered Flavian. "The great explorer heading off to certain disaster!"

Gribley finished strapping the luggage to the

roof rack of the big old black car they'd been lent for the journey, then did a final check that Fintan hadn't forgotten anything. Luckily the only things he'd forgotten were his passport and his rucksack, so it didn't take long to go back for them. As the car pulled away with Gribley at the wheel, Fintan's parents waved cheerily and his siblings pulled stupid faces.

"So, off we go then!" beamed Fintan. He happily unfolded the enormous map he'd brought along, elbowing Gribley in the head and causing him to knock over an ornamental flowerpot and take a chunk out of the peacock-shaped bush.

"What on earth's going on?" demanded Mrs Bumstead, climbing down from her tree branch when her bedraggled son came limping back towards her. "Why didn't you get him? I just saw him driving off with his butler! You let him get away!"

Eric wasn't in the mood for arguing. He wasn't in the mood for much else either, but managed to haul himself back over the wall and hobbled back to their parked car.

"Hurry up!" shouted Edith, getting into the passenger seat. "We can catch up with him if you get a move on!"

Eric carefully picked a few large chunks of broken glass from his coat sleeves, then took his place behind the wheel. The roar of agony that followed was loud enough to crack one of the car's wing mirrors and steam up Mrs Bumstead's glasses. Gritting his teeth, Eric leapt up and removed the huge spiky cactus from the seat of his trousers, then hurled it out of the window.

"What did you bring that thing for?" hollered Edith. "Stop wasting time and start driving, will you!"

With a spinning of tyres, a grinding of gears and the gnashing of Eric's teeth, the Bumsteads eventually headed off in hot pursuit.

Half a mile ahead, Fintan was attempting to refold the enormous map, which he had just discovered was of North Africa, so wasn't of much use for the drive to the airport. For some reason he couldn't fathom, it wouldn't fold quite as neatly as it should, so he ended up with a sort of large lumpy thing, crumpled into a ball.

"Fancy a sandwich yet, Gribs?" he said, happily tossing the map into the back seat and unzipping his rucksack.

"No, thank you, sir. I believe I can last a little longer," said Gribley coldly.

Fintan failed to notice the disapproving tone and produced a large peanut butter sandwich from an enormous pile he had stuffed into his bag. "Suit yourself, then. I'm famished!"

The fact that they had eaten an enormous farewell roast dinner not long before leaving home made Gribley doubt this statement, but he said nothing. Besides, he had become distracted by the sight in his rear-view mirror – a tatty little yellow car weaving around behind them. It appeared to be in a serious hurry and was trying desperately to pass.

"Quick! This is your chance!" bellowed Edith, as they came to an empty stretch of road with nothing but fields on either side. "Pull in front of him and you've got him trapped!"

Eric grinned like a madman, put his foot down and started accelerating past the black car in front. It was at that very moment that Fintan produced a flask from his rucksack and unscrewed the top.

"How about a nice hot cup of tea, then?" he asked, offering it to Gribley and spilling at least a cup's worth into his lap. Gribley let out a scream and took his hands off the steering wheel.

The inside of the car suddenly descended into frenzied chaos. Fintan started apologizing profusely for his clumsiness while attempting to mop up the mess with his hanky and spilling the rest of the tea on to the windscreen and his own shoes. Gribley was desperately trying to escape from his painfully hot, soaking-wet trousers and to see through the cloud of steam issuing from them.

The car veered out of control across the road, directly into the path of the Bumsteads' little yellow car, forcing Eric to swerve sharply to the right, off the road, through a wooden fence and into a field. Eric and Edith screamed in terror as their car bounced and skidded, deep in sloppy wet manure. A flock of startled chickens flapped into the air. Eric slammed on his brakes and juddered to a standstill.

A couple of the chickens, which had found their way in through an open window, fluttered and clucked and added to the already thick layer of dung coating the inside of the car.

"How could they have known?" shouted Edith after a few seconds of shocked silence. "How did they know about the plan?"

Eric scraped a handful of dung and chicken feathers from his face and scowled. This was getting serious! This rich kid wasn't the easy target he'd been expecting. The events of the last half hour now seemed to indicate that young Fintan Fedora was no ordinary kid. If anything, he was some sort of brilliant assassin!

"Don't just sit there sulking," yelled his mother, wiping the mess from her glasses. "Get after them! If they know about the plan, we can't let 'em get to the police!"

Eric revved the rattling engine, switched on his bent windscreen wipers and drove their battered little car unsteadily back on to the road. The Fedora's big black car was still just about visible in the distance, driving off as if nothing had happened.

As far as Fintan and Gribley knew, nothing had happened. In the chaos, they'd forgotten all about the yellow car behind them.

"I'm really, really sorry, Gribs!" Fintan was saying

as they drove on towards the airport. "I promise I'll be more careful from now on!"

Gribley didn't reply. They hadn't even left the country yet and he was already having serious regrets about the whole trip.

SIX

Two hours later, Gribley found himself in the gents' toilet at the airport, knocking on a locked cubicle door.

"Master Fedora, sir? Are you all right in there? We really must be hurrying along if we are to catch our flight..."

After a long pause and some nervous coughing, Fintan's small voice was heard from within.

"Er, yes, of course... I'll be out in a minute."

There was a further pause as Fintan decided that he couldn't hide in there all day and that maybe he'd better tell the truth. "Actually, I'm not feeling particularly keen about going on a plane at the moment, Gribley... I don't suppose we could sort of, you know, go on a ship or something, could we?"

Gribley had been expecting this. He knew very well about Fintan's fear of flying and had been wondering how long it would take for him to back out of the journey. The boy had only ever been on a plane once before in his life, which had turned out to be a traumatic experience for him. It had also been a terrifying experience for the pilot and the rest of the passengers, mostly because Fintan had smuggled a cat and several guinea pigs on board, which had escaped and chased each other up and down the plane for three hours.

"You do realize a sea voyage would take rather longer than an aeroplane, sir? It would be a matter of several days," said Gribley.

"Oh, that wouldn't be a problem, Gribs!" said Fintan from behind the door, suddenly sounding much chirpier. "It would be nice, I expect. Relaxing! Bit of sea air and all that!"

"Very well," sighed Gribley reluctantly, "I will make the necessary arrangements."

Before disappearing into the toilet, Fintan had spent a short time queueing nervously at the Brazil Airlines check-in desk. His state of mind hadn't been helped by the arrival of a very nasty-looking skinny old woman and a strange little fat man who smelled of manure and had cactus spines sticking out of his face. For some reason they had both stared intently at him as if they knew him, and worse still, as if they wanted to kill him. They had then watched him like hawks as he had nervously made his way to the loo, and he was pretty sure they had followed him there as well. Gribley had noticed them too, loitering awkwardly outside the toilets and shouting at each other. When he had gone to check on Fintan they had stopped arguing and begun whistling very badly as he passed. Strange people.

They were still there and had resumed their arguing through gritted teeth.

"Well, go on then! Get in there and do something!" said Edith, jabbing her son in the ribs. "This is our last chance! If they get on a plane we'll lose them!"

Eric wasn't quite ready to abandon all his hopes for gold-plated taps in the shape of swans, but he was a bit reluctant to be caught attempting a kidnap in such a public place.

"Don't be daft, Mother!" he hissed. "We can't just grab him with all these people around! Someone will notice! We need a clever plan."

At that moment something looking a bit like a clever plan walked right past them in the form of two airline cabin crew members.

"That's it!" said Eric, excited at his own cunning brilliance. "A disguise! We need to get some uniforms like those people! Then we can pretend we need to check the boy's passport or something. No one will suspect a thing! We ask him to come with us and bang, we've got him!"

Edith found herself surprisingly impressed by this idea. Mostly because she fancied wearing something which didn't stink quite so much of manure. "Yes!" she said with a sudden burst of excitement. "Uniforms! We need uniforms!"

Grinning broadly with their nasty yellow teeth, Edith and Eric abandoned their post outside the toilet door and began following the unsuspecting cabin crew.

Moments later Gribley and a much happier-looking Fintan emerged from the gents' with their suitcases, left the airport and headed for the coast.

Fintan and Gribley arrived at the Southampton docks without further incident, apart from almost colliding with a lorry load of peaches while driving on the wrong side of the road, and then going through a red traffic light and narrowly missing a minibus full of football supporters who had shouted some very rude words. Things had improved considerably when Gribley had finally persuaded Fintan to sit in the back seat and to stop interfering with the steering wheel.

Their ship, the *Magnifico*, was an impressively huge shiny white thing with hundreds of cabins, seven restaurants, three swimming pools and a cinema.

This is a much better way to travel than by a rotten old aeroplane, thought Fintan as he was shown to his cabin by a polite man in a smart white uniform. It had all the comforts he could possibly want and a few more he hadn't even thought of. This was a lot like being at home, except with the sea all around them! In fact, it was even better than being at home, because his disapproving parents and his irritating older brother and annoying older sister weren't around to pick on him!

"If there's anything I can do for you, sir, please don't hesitate to ask," said the man in the white uniform. Fintan grinned like a kid in a sweetshop.

"Brilliant!" he said. "Can I have a peanut butter sandwich, please?"

A much less enthusiastic Gribley was also shown into the cabin, where he piled up their enormous stack of luggage, sat on his bunk and prepared himself for several miserable days of seasickness.

SEVEN

Meanwhile, back at the airport, the Bumsteads were putting their new plan into action. They had spent a few frustrating minutes following their targets around, waiting for an opportunity to pounce. There always seemed to be too many people around. Eventually the air steward and stewardess turned into a quiet corridor and paused to talk outside an unlocked store cupboard. The Bumsteads leapt into action. With a flurry of pushing and shoving, they hurriedly bundled their victims into the cupboard and overpowered them. Not so much overpowering them by force, but by surprise, and by the revolting pong they were giving off.

"Give us yer uniforms, you!" snarled Edith.

"Yeah!" added Eric, menacingly pointing his finger and pretending it was a gun.

Amazingly, the terrified pair did what they were told. Eric pointed his finger gun at them while his mother tied them up with the cable from a floor-polishing machine and gagged them with dirty cleaning cloths. The cloths stank horribly, but not as badly as the Bumsteads.

Moments later, they emerged guiltily from the cupboard and locked the door behind them. The uniforms, of course, didn't fit. Eric's jacket was so small that he could barely do the buttons up across his fat stomach, while Edith's hung down to her knees and the sleeves covered her hands. Neither of them had managed to do their ties up properly and they were both still wearing their grimy old trainers. The additional fact that they still smelled very strongly of dung and that Eric looked like he'd recently fallen into a greenhouse full of cacti didn't help the authenticity of the disguises either. Worse still, they looked absolutely nothing like the photos on their security passes. Eric found a felt pen in his jacket pocket and made a few hasty alterations, which didn't help. However, they'd have to do, he thought. With luck, no one would look at them too closely.

"Right, then," he said, rubbing his hands with anticipation, "all we have to do now is find him and he's ours!"

After an hour of wandering around the check-in area scouring the crowds for a glimpse of Fintan, this optimism began to fade a little.

"They've got to be here somewhere!" snarled Eric. "We know they're going to Brazil because we saw them queueing to check their bags in! They must have gone through to the departure lounge or something."

Edith crossed her arms, rolled her eyes and sneered. "Oh, well, in that case we've lost them, haven't we! How are we supposed to go through the departure gate without a plane ticket? I don't know why I ever listen to your stupid ideas, I really don't!"

Eric tapped the side of his nose with a dung-stained finger. "No, we haven't lost them, Mother!" he whispered. "We've got these brilliantly convincing disguises on, remember? We're cabin crew! We can go through without a ticket and no one will take any notice!"

Trying not to look too self-conscious, the Bumsteads shuffled over to where the tickets were being checked. Taking a deep breath and thrusting their hands into their pockets to look even more casual, they began humming an out-of-tune version of "Come Fly With Me" and walked nonchalantly through the gate.

"There! You see!" said Eric triumphantly when they reached the other side. "No problem at all! Piece of cake! We've definitely got him now!"

They were just debating whether to stick together or to split up and search separately when they were interrupted by a loud, angry voice.

"You two!" it barked. "Where on earth do you think you're going looking like that?"

Someone with a red face and a big curly moustache who looked suspiciously like a pilot was striding towards them waving a clipboard.

Eric froze with fright. "Er, Brazil?" he muttered uncertainly.

"I was beginning to think you weren't going to turn up at all! And look at the state of you both, for goodness' sake! Smarten yourselves up at once!"

Edith looked at the floor like a schoolgirl being

41

told off and fiddled with her badly knotted tie. Eric smoothed down his horrible greasy hair with his dirty hands, which didn't make it look any better.

"Er, OK. . . Sorry," he mumbled guiltily, and then as an afterthought added, "Sir."

The pilot looked thoroughly unimpressed with his new recruits, but was apparently desperate enough to put up with them. "Hurry up and get yourselves on board, you scruffy pair. There are passengers to greet!"

Less than an hour later, the pair of supposed kidnappers found themselves at thirty thousand feet over the Atlantic, serving endless cups of tea and coffee to everyone on board. After they'd pushed their wobbly trolleys up and down the aisle a few times, it eventually dawned on them that Fintan wasn't on the plane, a discovery which meant they didn't smile quite as much as cabin crew are supposed to, and swore considerably more.

EIGHT

Thirty thousand feet below them, Fintan was enjoying his Atlantic cruise enormously. The food in the restaurants was excellent. There were movies to watch any time you felt like it, games arcades to lose your money in, souvenir shops where you could buy little plastic things you didn't need and numerous interesting passengers on board to chat to while leaning on the rail and watching the sea roll by. The crew would even make you peanut butter sandwiches and deliver them to your cabin at any hour of the day or night! Gribley, however, was having slightly less fun and had spent most of his time on deck desperately breathing in the sea air and trying not to be sick. He looked at his watch and sighed. If only they'd taken the plane they'd be in Brazil already. Instead he had to suffer several days of rolling seas and a horribly rolling stomach.

On his third very pleasant evening on board, Fintan strolled happily to the fanciest dining room looking forward to another large, excellent meal. This particular evening he found himself seated opposite a very tall American man with a shaved head, a neat little goatee, a gold earring and a very expensive-looking suit. The man confidently ordered an extremely expensive meal of caviar, something called lobster thermidor and an even more expensive bottle of vintage wine. Fintan decided to go for the sausages, chips and chocolate milk.

The American man reached across the table and shook Fintan's hand as if he were trying to squash it.

"The name's Wrench," he announced loudly. "Max Wrench. Call me Max!"

"Oh, OK," said Fintan as his hand was enthusiastically crushed in the man's big meaty paw. "I'm Fintan ... you can call me Fintan... I'm going to Brazil," he added, attempting to make polite conversation.

"Hey, you don't say! Me too!" laughed Mr

Wrench. "That's kinda lucky, cos that's where the ship's going! Ha haaa!"

There followed a short awkward silence, during which Fintan stuffed his mouth with chips and Max Wrench wondered whether he could go and sit at another table and avoid talking to this little English idiot for the duration of his fancy dinner.

"Are you on your holidays, Mr Wrench?" asked Fintan, eventually.

"Yup, sure am," said the man, through a mouthful of lobster. "I'm on vacation with Mrs Wrench, my good lady wife. We've done Europe; now we're gonna go stay at the biggest, most expensive hotel in Rio! Then we're gonna tour a few of the islands, do a little scuba-diving, pick up a few expensive souvenirs, do a little sunbathing on the yacht, you know..."

Fintan didn't know but nodded enthusiastically as if he did.

"Where is your wife, Mr Wrench – er, I mean, Max? Isn't she having any dinner?"

"Dinner? No way, poor Barbara's in her cabin. She gets seasick."

"Ah, I know what you mean!" said Fintan. "My

butler Gribley's got the same problem! Hates sea travel! Poor man's got absolutely no appetite. In fact, I wouldn't be surprised if he was throwing up over the side as we speak. Sick flying everywhere, I expect!"

Wrench stopped chewing his lobster for a moment and tried not to picture sick flying everywhere.

"How about you, kid? You on vacation too?" he asked, attempting to change the subject.

"Well, not really; it's more a sort of a business trip. I'm in the cake business, you see."

Wrench appeared pleased to hear this. Mainly because he was also in the cake business and it would give him a chance to show off. "Hey, really? Me too! I'm head of marketing strategies with Mommy's Yummy Cake Co, part of Giganti-Foods International! The biggest cake producer in the world! You must have heard of us!"

Fintan hadn't but nodded anyway.

"Guess that makes us rivals, eh?" snorted Mr Wrench, devouring his expensive dinner and laughing at the silliness of the idea.

Fintan felt the need to stick up for his family's business. "Oh. I'm head of, er . . . cake . . . things . . .

at Fedora Fancies," he lied, trying to sound impressive. ". . . UK."

"Yeah? Never heard of 'em!" sniggered Wrench.

Fintan decided he didn't like this man at all. He was rude and big-headed and loud, and he chewed with his mouth open! Worst of all, though, he was sitting there in his fancy suit with his silly beard treating Fintan as a silly kid who didn't belong in the world of business! How dare he!

Fintan felt a sudden need to show off too.

"I shouldn't tell you this, really," he began, leaning forward and lowering his voice, "but we're going on a secret expedition into the jungle. We're searching for the rare chocoplum fruit."

Max Wrench put down his knife and fork and stared at him with an amazed expression.

"No way! You're kidding, right?" he said, awestruck, and laughed a little too loudly for Fintan's taste. "The chocoplum! Ha ha! You dummy! That's just a kid's story!"

Fintan found this remark very insulting. He wasn't a kid and didn't like being called a dummy! He had it on very good authority that the chocoplum was real! He'd read about it in *Young Adventurer* magazine, which he'd been reading for years. *Young Adventurer* didn't write stories that weren't true!

"Hell, if the chocoplum were real, I'd know about it!" continued Wrench, between bursts of laughter. "I've been in the cake business thirty years and I know everything there is to know! I tell you, if the chocoplum were real, you can bet there'd be a Giganti-Foods International chocoplum range at the top of the market! Ha ha! In search of the rare chocoplum! You're funny, kid!"

Fintan poked sulkily at his chips and tried to ignore the man showing off. He reached for the ketchup bottle and accidentally knocked over Wrench's expensive vintage wine. The whole bottleful sloshed on to the table and flooded the man's plate of caviar and lobster thermidor.

NINE

The following evening, Fintan was out on the deck taking a bracing walk. The wind was blowing hard and the canvas covers on the lifeboats were flapping noisily. The sea heaved relentlessly up and down in the darkness. On his second lap of the enormous deck he came to the stern of the ship and saw Gribley gripping the handrail and leaning over the side.

"Hello, Gribs old man!" he shouted, over the noise of the wind and the crashing waves. "Still feeling a bit rough, eh?"

Gribley turned his very grey-looking face towards him and forced a nod of the head.

"Poor old you! Still, not long now! We should be there in another couple of days!"

Gribley smiled weakly and wished Fintan would keep his cheerful remarks to himself. "Mind you don't lean over too far, Gribs, you might fall in!" Fintan hollered wittily as Gribley returned his attention to being sick.

"You must be ever so hungry by now," he continued. "Can I get you anything? I had some lovely sausages and chips again tonight! Nice and greasy, just how I like them!"

Suddenly Fintan felt someone slapping him heartily on the back. "Hey, kid! How's it going?" boomed Wrench's annoying loud voice.

Fintan turned round. "Oh, I'm OK, thanks," he said. "Sorry about your lobster thermostat. It was an accident, honest it was."

The man waved a hand to indicate it was nothing. He had easily afforded a replacement dinner and another bottle of wine. "So! Have you found the legendary chocoplum yet?" he boomed, apparently still finding the idea hilarious.

At that point Gribley decided he'd heard quite enough about greasy food and lobsters. He shuffled unsteadily away below deck in search of a toilet. He wouldn't feel any less sick in there but at least he wouldn't have to listen to Fintan "cheering him up" any more.

The American man was still laughing at his own joke. "Hey, when you find 'em, make sure you let me know, OK? When you're a chocoplum millionaire! Or who knows, maybe I might just get there first and beat you to it! Ha ha haaa!"

It may have been meant as a joke but Fintan didn't find it very funny.

"Chocoplums!" snorted the man. "You wait until I tell the guys back home about this!"

Fintan watched as the annoying man strolled away to the opposite side of the ship, laughing loudly to himself.

It was only then that he noticed Gribley had gone. Fintan stared blankly at the railing where he had been standing. There was no sign of him! The wind whipped sharply around his head and the dark sea sloshed around in a mess of spray, but there was no Gribley.

He's fallen in! thought Fintan with a sudden cold dread. *Gribley's fallen in!* For a moment he just stared over the side in helpless panic, then started to run backwards and forwards in an even more helpless state of panic. He followed this by shouting "Man overboard!" at the top of his voice, even though no one could hear him. Suddenly he spotted a red and white lifebelt with *Magnifico* written on it on the ship's bulkhead, grabbed it, dashed back to the railing and hurled it into the darkness like a huge frisbee. Unfortunately, Fintan had thrown it directly into a gale-force wind, which immediately turned it round and hurled it backwards across the ship.

At that very moment, on the opposite side of the deck, Max Wrench was making a long-distance phone call to his boss at Giganti-Foods International in New York, keen to share the hilarious story he'd just been reminded of.

"Hey, Randall, it's me, Max!" he yelled, shielding the phone from the buffeting wind. "Yeah, yeah, it's pretty good! Having a real good time! Barbara's still kinda ill, but what you gonna do, huh? But hey, Randy, get this! You'll never guess what some stupid kid on the ship told me yesterday! Dumb kid thinks the chocoplum fruit story is true! Yeah! He really does! The idiot's actually going to Brazil in search of chocoplum trees!"

A long-distance tinny laugh issued from the earpiece of Max's phone as Randall T. Buckmeister, head of Giganti-Foods International, joined in with the fun.

"What did you say?" continued Wrench, still shouting into his phone. "Who is he? He's a nobody! Works for some scrawny little no-hope cake business called 'Fe-boring Fancy' or something! I think he's actually scared I'm going to follow him! What's he gonna do, kill me? Ha ha!"

At that precise moment a red and white lifebelt with *Magnifico* written on it smacked into the back of Max Wrench's big bald head, hurling him over the railing and down into the sea, where he disappeared with a muffled splash. Gasping for breath and shocked witless, he surfaced and grabbed hold of a trailing length of rope. Luckily for him, the lifebelt had caught on a bracket protruding from the side of the ship.

"HELP!!" he spluttered as he was dragged along up to his neck in freezing sea water. With his free hand, Max groped in his soggy pockets for his phone, but realized it must be heading for the bottom of the ocean. On the other end of the phone line, Randall T. Buckmeister was still laughing, but wondering why there had been a loud thud followed by a strange gurgling noise.

Still in a state of utter confusion, Fintan rushed down the ship's corridor shouting "Man overboard!" in a hysterical voice. Several elderly passengers came out of their cabins to see what all the commotion was about and were knocked flying as he rushed past. Three uniformed members of the crew managed to catch up with him and attempted to calm him down a little.

"Sir, sir," said one of the men, shaking him by his shoulders and staring into his face. "Please try and remain calm, sir. We need you to tell us exactly what has happened."

"He fell in!" shrieked Fintan, not calming down much at all. "Poor old Gribs fell in!"

One of the other men joined in. "You need to stop panicking and focus, sir. Tell us exactly where he fell. . ."

"In the sea!" wailed Fintan, thinking that much should be pretty obvious.

The crew immediately went into well-rehearsed action. The tallest and most bearded of them began hauling Fintan back out on to the deck to identify where they should search, while the second sent a "code red" to the captain by radio and the third set about calming the other passengers who had gathered to join in with the panic. On the ship's bridge, a deafening hooting alarm was sounded and an emergency signal was sent to the engine room to stop all engines. Red lights flashed. The chief engineer stopped doing his crossword, leapt to his feet and set about instructing the assistant engineers in the shut-down procedure. Men in boiler suits ran clattering along suspended metal walkways shouting and turning valve wheels. Heavy iron pipes groaned with sudden changes in pressure and the needles on all the dials flipped madly from side to side. Within a few seconds both the ship's massive steam turbine engines began to slow and the massive eighty-five-thousand-ton bulk of the *Magnifico* shuddered violently to a halt.

Up on deck, the first mate, several other crew members and a large group of passengers had gathered excitedly around Fintan, who was pointing to the spot where he had last seen Gribley standing. More men dressed in heavy waterproof clothing appeared hurriedly on the scene, blew whistles and began lowering one of the ship's lifeboats over the side.

"You're quite sure it was here? Definitely this side?" asked the first mate, who was worried that the gibbering wreck in front of him may not be a very reliable witness.

Fintan nodded and looked stricken with terror.

"You're quite sure?" continued the first mate.

Fintan nodded again.

"And can you tell me who it was that you saw fall overboard?"

"Yes," said Fintan. "It was him." He pointed a trembling finger at Gribley, who was standing at the back of the crowd, wondering what on earth was happening. The assembled crowd fell quiet, then turned and stared at the ashen-faced man in a formal black suit who had just returned from the loo.

"I beg your pardon?" said the first mate.

"Yes, that's him!" said Fintan clearly. "That's the man who fe…"

The crew weren't sure whether to be relieved or furious and settled for being a bit of both as they watched Fintan run over to the man and seize him in a frenzied hug.

"Thank goodness you're all right, Gribs!" squeaked Fintan. "I thought you'd fallen in the sea!" Gribley looked astonished but was more concerned that the sudden dramatic hug was making him feel horribly sick again.

The crew set about cancelling the lifeboat launch and dispersing the crowd. Messages were sent to the bridge and the engine room that it had all been a false alarm and that no one had actually fallen overboard at all. Fintan spent a few minutes apologizing profusely to everyone and a few more minutes being lectured by the first mate for his irresponsible behaviour. He felt thoroughly silly and ashamed but also hugely relieved that poor old Gribley hadn't gone to a watery grave after all. When the lecture and the apologies were over, they slowly made their way back below deck. For a brief moment Fintan thought he heard the wind carry a man's voice shouting for help, but put it down to his heightened imagination. *Emergencies can do strange things to your senses*, he told himself, and headed back to his cabin.

TEN

"Well, what a stupid idea that was!" snarled an exhausted Edith Bumstead, as she trudged out of the airport into the darkness of a Brazilian evening. "Let's disguise ourselves as cabin crew, says my criminal mastermind son! We can ask the boy for his passport! Brilliant! And what did we get? Eleven hours of serving tea and having to be nice to people, that's what! Don't think I'm going to forget this in a hurry, young man, because I won't!"

"Oh shut up moaning, will you!" snapped Eric, who wasn't feeling particularly cheerful either. "It's not my fault they weren't on the plane, is it! All I know is the boy's obviously a lot cleverer than we thought."

Feeling extremely sorry for themselves, the failed

kidnappers slouched over to a wooden bench just outside the airport and slumped miserably on to it. The fact that they had just got a free ride to one of the most beautiful and exciting locations in the world didn't even occur to them. They weren't in the mood for looking on the bright side. The memory of being outsmarted by some horrible spoilt little kid was still far too painful to allow them any happy thoughts. So was the even more recent memory of being exposed as fake cabin crew, sacked for gross incompetence and unceremoniously thrown off the plane as soon as it hit the tarmac.

"And we didn't even get paid!" said Edith bitterly. "What a cheek!"

Eric nodded in mute agreement and scuffled his feet around in the dust. Several minutes passed in awkward silence, broken only by the occasional sigh and Edith removing her smelly trainers to rub her aching feet.

"So what are we supposed to do now, Mister Clever Clogs?" she said eventually. "We've got no money, no food, no passports and we don't speak . . . er . . . whatever language it is they speak here!"

Eric attempted to pull a face which would make

him look less stupid. "Don't you worry, Mum. That Fintan Fedora may be clever, but he's not clever enough to get the better of me! I'm working on a new plan already."

He paused awhile for effect, then announced, "I reckon we should wait right here! We should do a stake-out."

Unsurprisingly, Edith was unimpressed with this new plan. She sneered and made a noise like a horse exhaling.

"No, listen," continued Eric. "They're bound to be on the next flight, aren't they. They reckon they've given us the slip, but that's where they're wrong! They won't be expecting us to be waiting around for them here!"

Neither Eric nor Edith thought this was much of a plan, but it did at least mean they wouldn't have to do anything for a while, which was a good enough reason for Edith going along with it. Four hours passed, and night fell. Crickets chirped noisily in the bushes. Every now and then a small cluster of people emerged from the airport and headed to the car park or got into a waiting cab. None of them were Fintan Fedora.

"I'm hungry," announced Eric, after a few more hours of sitting in the dark. He rummaged through his pockets, found a couple of stale bread rolls he'd stolen from the in-flight catering trolley and bit ravenously into one.

"Give us some," said his mother, still rubbing her stinky old feet.

"What? Why should I?" moaned Eric, spraying her with little lumps of flaky crust. "You should've got your own like I did!"

"You selfish little pig!" hollered Edith, whose temper had been getting steadily worse for some time. Eric stuffed his mouth even fuller and clutched both rolls protectively to his chest.

"Forward planning, Mother, forward planning!" he spluttered. "I can't help it if you're too thick to plan ahead, can I!"

He would probably have said more, but at that point his mother's bony old fist hit him squarely in the face. He fell off the bench and coughed a huge mouthful of damp bread on to the ground.

"Selfish! That's what you are!" continued Edith furiously, leaping on to his back and rubbing his face into the dusty ground. "Totally selfish!"

Eric rolled over, bucking like a horse, and knocked his mother head first into the bench. Her glasses flew off into the bushes.

"Oh yeah? Selfish, am I?" he yelled while trying to get his mother in a stranglehold. "Well, at least I'm not thick like you!"

For the next few minutes mother and son traded insults and swung their fists at each other. Eventually, when they were both too exhausted to fight any more, they sat miserably at either end of the bench picking at what was left of the bread rolls, nursing their black eyes and dabbing at their nosebleeds with grubby hankies. Dawn began to break and the air temperature began to rise. Still there was no sign of Fintan.

"So how much longer are we going to wait here?" ventured Edith, finally breaking the unpleasant silence between them. Eric shrugged his shoulders sulkily and said nothing, preoccupied with a loose tooth he'd just discovered.

An hour later the heat and the boredom became unbearable. Reluctantly they got up and began trudging along the dusty road towards the nearest town.

ELEVEN

The *Magnifico* sailed grandly into port in blazing South American sunshine.

"Looks like we made it then, Gribs old man!" beamed Fintan, as he crammed his rucksack with a new stock of peanut butter sandwiches he'd had made up, just in case they didn't have them in Brazil. "One step closer to the chocoplum, eh?"

Gribley was still unconvinced of this, but he agreed anyway, out of politeness. Once the ship had docked, the passengers began to disembark in an excited throng, weighed down with suitcases, brightly coloured sun hats and noisy children. Amongst the crowd an anxious-looking American woman with oversized sunglasses was rushing around asking everyone whether they might have seen her missing husband. No one had.

Gribley walked ashore, pushing their large trolley-load of luggage and looking hugely relieved to be back on dry land. Even more relieved to be on dry land, however, was Max Wrench. Exhausted, wrinkled as a prune and covered in seaweed, he emerged from the sea and hauled himself on to the quayside. He lay there face down for a while trying to find the strength to stand.

"Are you all right, sir?" enquired one of the white-uniformed crewmen, gazing down at his horribly sunburnt bald head. Wrench opened one eye and looked absolutely furious.

"No, I am NOT all right!" he croaked.

The man was just helping him to his feet when Barbara Wrench spotted him and came rushing over.

"Where on earth have you been hiding?" she demanded. "Do you know how ill I've been for the past few days? Do you? I've just had to suffer the worst days of my life holed up in that rotten excuse for a ship!"

Max tried to interrupt her flow of angry

accusations but was feeling too weak. "I have been so sick, Max!" she continued. "So sick you wouldn't believe! And where were you, huh? Were you there to hold my hand and keep me company like any decent husband? Oh no! You were nowhere to be seen! Probably in the bar with your pals or in the restaurant stuffing yourself with fancy food! Not one shred of sympathy for your poor suffering wife who—"

"Shut up, Barbara!" rasped Wrench, his eyes bulging like a madman. "Not now, OK, not now! Gimme your phone, I need to make an urgent call."

Barbara was shocked into silence for a moment, but it wasn't long before she found her voice again.

"How dare you talk to me like that!" she shrieked. "You are the rudest, nastiest, most selfish man..."

Ignoring his wife's continuing list of his failings, he grabbed her handbag, rifled through it and pulled out her mobile phone. Max poked clumsily at the keypad with his numb, wrinked fingers and was relieved to get straight through to his boss in New York.

"Randall, it's Wrench," he said hurriedly, in a voice made croaky from three days and nights in the sea, shouting for help. "Now listen, this is important! I'm not fooling around here. You know that dumb kid I was talking about? Well, he tried to kill me! I swear! He whacked me over the head! Knocked me into the ocean and left me for dead! This kid is really serious! He's a killer!"

"What?" said Randall T. Buckmeister from his luxurious New York office. "What do you mean, he tried to kill you? Are you insane? Why would he do that?"

"Think about it, Randall," continued Wrench. "It's the chocoplums! Last thing I said to the kid was that I might get there first and beat him to it. It was a joke, Randall! I thought the whole thing was a joke until he attacked me. But now . . . I'm thinking it must be true! He knows where the chocoplums are!"

Recently, he'd been thinking about nothing else. Being knocked into the ocean and having to cling on to the end of a rope for three days and nights can have that effect on a person.

Four thousand miles to the north, Randall put

down his big smelly cigar in amazement. "This is perfect, Max!" he shouted excitedly, showing even less sympathy than Barbara had. "If this is true, it's worth a fortune! We must beat him to it! Whatever you do, don't lose sight of him!"

Wrench began to hurry through the crowd on his unsteady legs, barging holiday-makers out of the way and craning his neck for a view of Fintan. "I see him!" he hissed into his phone. "He's with some older guy and they're getting into a cab."

"Excellent! Read me the licence plate and I'll put some of our local guys right on to it!"

Wrench hurriedly dictated the taxi's number into his phone, then ended the call and stood swaying slightly from all the sudden exertion. Gradually a mixture of dehydration, sunburn, hunger and exhaustion caught up with him. He wobbled a bit, went cross-eyed and fainted backwards on to the quayside.

A few hundred yards away, Fintan and Gribley were piling their odd assortment of luggage into the back of a taxi. "Er ... Santos Coelho... town centre ... hotel, please, driver..." said Fintan, whose knowledge of foreign languages was about as poor as his knowledge of everything else. "Understandy? Hotello?"

The taxi driver stared blankly at him and shrugged. Gribley decided he'd better help out.

"Allow me, sir," he said. *"Um hotel agradável no centro de cidade de Santos Coelho por favor, excitador,"* which roughly translates as "A nice hotel in Santos Coelho town centre please, driver."

"Ah! *Sim, senhor,*" said the taxi driver, who seemed to have understood perfectly well, as he drove off straight away in a cloud of dust.

Fintan was thoroughly impressed and just as confused. "Good lord, Gribley! I didn't know you spoke Spanish!"

Gribley smiled modestly. "I took the precaution of bringing along a phrasebook. And it's not Spanish, sir, it's Portuguese. It's the language the inhabitants of Brazil speak."

"Really? Well, fancy that! Shouldn't they speak Brazilian or something?"

As it turned out, Gribley had just enough time to explain a few hundred years of international history before the cab arrived in Santos Coelho town. They unloaded their belongings and checked into a small whitewashed hotel without Fintan breaking anything, which by his standards was a pretty good sign.

TWELVE

After a good night's sleep in proper beds with no seasickness, the intrepid explorers ate a hearty breakfast and prepared to start the next stage of their expedition.

"Master Fintan, sir," said Gribley tentatively as they walked down the stairs into the hotel lobby, "now that we're here, may I ask how you intend to locate these precious fruits – assuming, of course, they exist?"

"They exist all right, Gribs!" Fintan said confidently. "They grow in the rainforest! It says so in *Young Adventurer*." He brandished a crumpled copy of his magazine, which he had brought with him for reference purposes.

"Indeed," continued Gribley, "but I understand

the Brazilian rainforest to be rather large, sir. In the region of seven million square kilometres."

"Is it?" replied Fintan. He raised an eyebrow and whistled. "Wow, that's pretty big! Good job I brought my walking boots, then! The thing is, you see, Gribs, we need to find this old lady who was in the magazine article. She lives round here. Says she saw them when she was a little girl and knows exactly where they are!"

Gribley looked at the photograph Fintan was showing him and his heart sank a little further. The woman looked about a hundred years old! *Oh dear*, he thought to himself, *this is worrying. The poor old thing's probably completely mad! She either made it up or imagined it, and even if she was telling the truth, the last time she saw the trees was about ninety years ago! What are the chances that they'd still be there?* He said nothing but forced a fairly encouraging nod of the head.

Fintan walked to the reception desk and rang the bell with a confident slap of the hand. The bell broke and rolled on to the floor with a loud clatter. Used to such little problems, Fintan casually pushed it out of sight with his foot. After a moment a receptionist arrived at the desk wearing a smart purple jacket, a little black moustache and a wide professional grin.

"Can I help you, *senhor*?" he beamed, through his strong local accent.

"Ah, yes, please!" said Fintan, holding his magazine open at the chocoplum article and pointing at the photograph of the old woman. "I'm looking for the lady in this picture. She's called Correntina or something ... I can't pronounce her second name at all, I'm afraid."

The man produced his reading glasses from his top pocket, put them on and stared intently at the picture.

"Ah, yes, *senhor*," he announced, "Correntina Cavalcanti. This lady is known to me! She very well known lady here in Santos Coelho. Very good cook at Café Gordurosa in town. Five minutes walkings from here."

"Really? Brilliant!" said Fintan, amazed at how easy this was turning out to be. "Do you think you could draw me a little map, please?"

Armed with this encouraging information and a rough map scribbled on the back of the magazine,

Fintan and Gribley walked out of the lobby into the street, leaving the receptionist looking at his desk and wondering where the bell had gone.

The air outside was hot and thick and smelled of several things at once. Exotic blossoms, strange meaty things on sticks being sold by people from little carts, car exhaust fumes and overflowing rubbish bins being rummaged through by skinny stray dogs. Children in shorts and sandals were running around shouting excitedly; car horns honked and church bells rang. Fintan thought it was brilliant.

"Isn't this brilliant, Gribs!" he said, to demonstrate his point. "We really are in a foreign country now, aren't we! Everything's different! And best of all, we know where to find Correntina already! I've got a feeling this is going to be great!"

With Fintan in charge of the map-reading, they strode contentedly off in search of Café Gordurosa through narrow, noisy streets lined with banana trees and old, brightly coloured buildings with peeling paint. Almost everything they saw was new, strange and amazing. They watched as gaudily painted buses struggled up steep hills, frightening the occasional chicken wandering around on the cobbles. They passed makeshift homes made of corrugated iron and old packing cases with endless lines of washing hanging out in the sun. Neither of them, however, noticed when a man in dark glasses with a large black beard began to follow them. Whenever they stopped to check where they were, the man stopped too, leant against a wall and pretended to be reading his newspaper. Fintan probably still wouldn't have noticed him even if he'd been wearing a large bright-orange hat with SPY written on it.

Just over an hour later, Fintan began to doubt whether the café really was only "five minutes walkings" away.

"Perhaps if you'd let me read the map, sir..." suggested Gribley. He was handed the crumpled magazine, which Fintan had been rotating, trying to make sense of the simple directions. Once they'd retraced their steps for a while, they found themselves outside a small tatty-looking building with old wrought-iron balconies and crumbling reddish plaster. A hand-painted sign over the door read "Café Gordurosa".

"Aha! Here we are then!" announced Fintan happily, and opened the door with his hopes high.

The café was cramped, dimly lit and smelled strongly of strange spices. There were a handful of tables strewn with dirty plates and empty bottles, and a crackly radio was playing old-fashioned Latino music. Several elderly women in big hats were sitting in old wooden chairs arguing loudly with each other in Portuguese.

When Fintan and Gribley walked in, the chatter abruptly stopped. Every eye in the place turned and stared at the strange-looking pair. An awkward silence fell, broken only by the distorted tune coming from the radio and a wonky old ceiling fan that creaked painfully above them.

Fintan looked like a small deer caught in the headlights of an oncoming truck. He smiled weakly and held up the picture of Correntina Cavalcanti. Without saying a word or changing their distrustful expressions, several of the old ladies pointed towards an open door that led to a dark, smoky kitchen. Both Gribley and Fintan nodded in mute understanding and quietly walked over to it. Fintan called out an exploratory "hello" and waited for a reply.

From the dark kitchen they could hear what sounded like someone chopping through chunks of gristle with a large cleaver and things sizzling in pans. Eventually the chopping noises stopped and a tiny, extremely wrinkly old woman appeared behind the counter. Her hair was white, wiry and as thin as candyfloss. She was wearing the tattiest dress and the filthiest apron Fintan had ever seen, neither of which appeared to have been anywhere near a washing machine in several years. She was clutching a large metal skewer on which was impaled a lump of raw, red meat, dripping blood and grease on to the floor. She squinted at her two visitors, eyeing them up and down as if they were aliens. It appeared she wasn't going to ask them what they wanted, so Gribley coughed slightly and gestured for Fintan to explain why they were there.

"Er, Mrs Correntina?" he began tentatively. "You are Mrs Correntina, yes? You lady in magazine?" At this point he thought it would be easier to spread his crumpled copy of *Young Adventurer* on the counter than to attempt miming what a magazine was. The old woman peered at the article through glassy-looking yellow eyes and a flicker of understanding appeared on her face. Fintan felt encouraged and stabbed his index finger at his chest. "Me from

England," he said, very slowly and distinctly. "Er. . .
Me look for chocoplum tree." Performing a mime
of what a tree looked like struck him as being a
useful addition at this point, so he stretched his
arms up like he remembered doing at nursery
school. Correntina still said nothing but now stared
at him as if he weren't just an alien but a very stupid
alien. "Where – is – yummy – fruit?" he went on,
taking care to say each word very clearly. As if this
wasn't enough, he imitated what he thought looked
like someone eating fruit, then rubbed his belly and
made yummy noises. Gribley stared at the floor,
horribly embarrassed by this amateurish attempt at
international communication.

"I'm not stupid, you know!" said Correntina
suddenly. "I do speak English."

Fintan looked extremely relieved. "Oh, that's
good then!" he announced.

Correntina wiped her hands on her dirty apron
and placed the dead thing on the counter. "Come,"
she said, shuffling out into the café and pointing to
a vacant table, "we'd better talk."

By now the level of the voices in the café had
returned to their previous passionate pitch, so it

looked like they would have to talk fairly loudly too. The three of them sat at a wooden table, which Correntina wiped clear of unidentifiable crumbs and lumps with her wrinkled old hand. The café door opened again and a man in dark glasses with a huge bushy black beard strolled in without attracting any interest at all. He walked to the counter, ordered a strong coffee from a young spotty man who had appeared from the kitchen, then sat at the adjacent table and disappeared behind his newspaper.

"I should have known this would happen," said Correntina. She shook her head sorrowfully. "I shouldn't have said anything to that magazine reporter! We'll probably be overrun with people now!"

Fintan leant across the table and moved aside a wax-covered old bottle holding a stumpy candle so that he could talk more privately. "Oh no, I shouldn't think so!" he said. "In fact, most people don't even believe the chocoplum is real! I even met a man on the way here who laughed at me when I mentioned it! You needn't worry about people coming to bother you!"

"You came!" she said matter-of-factly.

"Ah, yes, good point!" added Fintan. "I suppose I did. But I'm sure no one else will!"

The old woman became silent again, apparently not reassured, and looked sadly at the magazine article.

"So..." continued Fintan, putting on his best friendly voice, "are you going to tell me where they are? ... I mean, please?"

Correntina sighed and looked dubious. "I'm not sure I can do that," she said.

"What? Why?" stammered Fintan, suddenly horrified that his quest had reached a dead end. "Don't you remember where they are?"

"Of course I remember!" snapped Correntina. "Like I said, I'm not stupid! But why should I trust you, eh? How do I know you won't take all the fruits away to your own country and spoil the forest with your big boots and your noisy chainsaws? You must understand that the chocoplum grove is a very special place for me. It's a secret place to my family, hidden in a beautiful tiny valley, hardly visited by anyone. My parents showed the grove to me when I was a little girl and I saw the fruits growing there. Each year on my birthday I was allowed to eat one." She paused and for a moment looked lost in a treasured memory. "Why did I ever speak to that magazine reporter! It will only bring trouble."

Gribley had been listening to the sad old woman speaking with some astonishment. Much to his surprise, she wasn't as mad as a sack of frogs, as he'd been expecting, but sounded distinctly like she knew what she was talking about! This was quite a revelation. Even more amazingly, it also meant that Fintan wasn't as daft as he'd thought either! That idea would take rather more getting used to.

"Madam Correntina," he said, having decided he ought to help out a little, "I can assure you that we have no intention of damaging the trees, or indeed of taking away all the fruit. We merely wish to acquire a small sample for planting. If the fruit can be grown in our own greenhouses, then it will be much less of a rarity and no one will need to disturb your valley."

Correntina must have found Gribley's words reassuring, because she suddenly looked a lot more comfortable. "If I tell you of this secret place, you must promise me not to cut any of the trees down. Or to pick all the fruit," she said cautiously.

Fintan nodded, moved the stubby candle on to the next table, and leant closer, eager to hear the secret location.

After a little more thought, Correntina decided she could trust them. At least, she decided she could trust the nice grown-up one in the suit. "My granddaughter Ana lives in a small village near the edge of the rainforest, a very long bus journey to the south. If you promise you will respect my wishes, I will arrange for her to show you the way."

Fintan's delight at hearing this news was interrupted by a sudden commotion from the next table, as the candle he'd just moved set fire to the bearded man's newspaper. The man let out a frightening shriek, then leapt up and flapped his burning paper in a futile attempt to extinguish it. The flames quickly spread to the man's black beard, which he hurriedly took off, threw to the floor and stamped on. This, and the nasty smell of burnt nylon in the air, led Fintan to believe that it might have been a false one.

"Sorry about that," said Fintan, awkwardly, "I just sort of moved the candle a bit ... to be safe, and, well, you know..."

The man didn't reply, but furiously adjusted his slightly melted sunglasses and stormed out into the street, leaving his newspaper and his fake beard smouldering away on the café floor.

"What a strange man!" said Fintan.

THIRTEEN

It was nearly lunchtime by the time the Bumsteads staggered into Santos Coelho town centre, though according to their stomachs, it was already several hours past lunchtime. Possibly several days. Edith had eaten a handful of berries she'd found in a roadside bush and was now regretting it, as they were causing severe stomach cramps and uncontrollable wind. The fact that the resulting wind smelled like rotting fish meant that Eric was regretting her eating them too. With their stolen jackets draped over their heads to keep the sun off, they slouched into town and looked around for somewhere to eat.

"So what's your next brilliant plan, then?" enquired Edith sarcastically. "We haven't got any money, remember?"

"Simple," said Eric. "We go to a café, order food and eat it. Before they bring the bill, we run for it. Just like we do when we eat out at home. Not having any foreign money is the same as not having any English money."

They stopped outside a classy-looking restaurant and peered in the window. "This'll do nicely!" pronounced Eric, and pushed the door open. Despite their shambolic appearance and unpleasant smell, a waiter politely seated them by the window and gave them both a large leather-bound menu.

"See!" said Eric smugly. "Piece of cake, as usual!"

The menu was, of course, written in Portuguese – but luckily there were also little illustrations, which they pointed at hungrily when the waiter returned. Having ordered two huge main courses each and three sticky desserts, they settled back in their chairs and happily awaited the free feast. Outside the restaurant window, the good people of Santos Coelho were going about their daily business. Fat-bellied men with big moustaches accompanied by smiling women with big hats ambled around casually in the sunshine. A shaven-headed man was happily selling delicious-looking hot dogs and tortillas from a rusty old green van. Next to this stood a small, busy bus station where a group of colourfully dressed people with suitcases was gathered. Most looked like locals, but there was also a handful of tourists. Eric's eyes fell on an extremely old woman in a dirty apron who was giving directions to a pair of Europeans. One was a smartly dressed man in his fifties and the other was a scruffy-haired boy who seemed to be dressed as a jungle explorer. Lurking furtively behind them was an odd-looking man in a terrible fake beard. He appeared to be fiddling about with the boy's rucksack, as if he were trying to hide something in it. Eric watched with vague interest. He could understand why someone might take things out of people's rucksacks. That was stealing. But putting things in? Very odd! He was just musing to himself how weird this was when he suddenly realized who the boy was. Eric's mouth fell open and he pointed in mute astonishment out of the window.

"I don't believe it!" he said when he finally recovered the power of speech. "Mum, look! Look, it's HIM! Standing at that bus stop!"

At that very moment a bus pulled up by the waiting passengers, obscuring their view.

"Who?" said Edith distractedly, far more interested in what was about to appear on her plate than anything that might be going on outside.

"It's the Fedora boy, look!" hissed Eric, who was already rising from his chair.

Edith looked where he was pointing and saw nothing but a bus. "Don't be so daft, Eric," she snapped. "You're seeing things again, aren't you?"

"It was definitely him! And the other bloke too, the butler! I know it!"

Without waiting to see if his mother was going to follow him or not, Eric bolted from the table and ran out into the street. Dodging the traffic, he rushed across the road and stared into the bus as each of the passengers took their seats. The scruffy-haired boy took a window seat right in front of him and immediately began eating the peanut butter sandwiches he'd packed for the journey. It was undoubtedly Fintan Fedora! Right in front of him! The horrible, irritating little kid Eric had been trying so hard to kidnap and who had outwitted him at every turn!

Edith emerged at the restaurant door and bellowed across the street at him: "Eric! Get back here! They're bringing the food. Eric! Are you even listening to me?"

The bus pulled away and Eric's blood boiled. Determined not to lose his quarry again, he ran after it for a while, then stopped and looked around frantically for some form of transport he could steal. With a look of insane intent on his face, he clambered into the open flap on the side of the hot dog van and began scuffling with its horrified owner. Edith hobbled towards the violently shaking van, screaming for Eric to pull himself together and come back for his lunch, but arriving just in time to see the poor innocent hot dog vendor get shoved out on to the road.

"Eric! What the hell do you think you're doing?" she shrieked.

"Shut up and get in, Mother!" Eric barked, starting the tatty old van's engine. Edith flung open the passenger door and awkwardly climbed in.

With a nasty squealing of tyres and crunching of gears, Eric steered the van away from its protesting owner at full speed and headed after the disappearing bus.

"Are you completely mad?" shouted Edith. "They were just bringing the food! It smelled really nice!"

"It was HIM, I tell you!" said Eric, through gritted teeth, his face red with rage and exhilaration. "It was definitely HIM!"

Ignoring the hail of bottles, sausages and frying pans which were flying out of the wide-open serving hatch, the Bumsteads roared out of Santos Coelho and headed south towards the forest. The chase was on again!

FOURTEEN

Max Wrench was sitting in his hotel room applying a soothing cream to his burnt head when the phone rang. He snatched it up immediately. "Wrench here. Any news?"

"Yes, but not good," replied Randall T. Buckmeister from his New York office. "I think you may be right. I had Gonzalez, one of our best Brazilian guys, look into this Fedora kid's background. His story checks out. He's serious. Gonzalez tailed him undercover to a rendezvous with an old woman at a café. Seems the kid realized he was being followed and . . . er, set fire to him."

"I knew it!" snarled Wrench, whose worst suspicions were now confirmed. "You see what we're up against here! Don't let his age fool you! He's ruthless!"

"Certainly looks that way," agreed Randall. "But it also means he's on to something big! Whoever this old woman was, she gave him some information. I've instructed Gonzalez to keep watch outside the kid's hotel. When he makes a move, we'll be right after him. Listen, Wrench, wherever these fruits are, I want you to get there first! Whatever it costs! I'll put all the company's resources at your disposal."

"You can trust me, Randall. I'll beat this kid to the fruit trees, all right!" said Wrench confidently, then after a moment or two's thought, began to reel off his shopping list. "First off, we're gonna need plenty of guns. Get me some armed guys on the ground. Tracking gear, satellite phones, helicopters with lifting facilities, forest-clearing machinery, flame-throwers, that kinda thing. Oh, and I'll need a bunch of cash too. This could get expensive."

Randall saw no problem with any of this. In the corrupt world of Giganti-Foods International, helicopters and flame-throwers were a fairly normal requirement. The cake business was a very serious affair. "Consider it done, Wrench," he barked, and hung up.

There was a brief nasty silence, during which

Wrench realized his wife Barbara was scowling at him.

"Oh I see, so it's suddenly turned into another business trip, has it, Max?" she sneered, with her hands planted angrily on her hips. "And what about the luxury holiday you promised to take me on? What about the sightseeing and the yachts and the shopping? If you think you're going to ruin MY holiday just to please that boss of yours, then you'd better think again! I'm warning you! If you're not careful, then this marriage is in serious trouble! It's me or the cakes, Max! Make your choice: me or the cakes!"

Max didn't have to think very hard about this dilemma.

"Have a nice holiday, Barb," he said, closing the door behind him.

FIFTEEN

"Good grief, Gribley! This country is enormous!" said Fintan, as he stared out of the bus window at the seemingly endless hills and forests streaming past them. "I thought England was big until I came here! This must be twice as big, at least!"

"I believe Brazil to be around thirty-five times larger than the United Kingdom, sir," said Gribley in his usual matter-of-fact tone. "The seventh largest land area in the world, in fact, covering in the region of 8,456,510 square kilometres."

Fintan whistled, apparently impressed. "Really? Amazing! How do you know all this stuff, Gribley?"

"I read it in books, sir."

"Books, eh? Clever!" nodded Fintan thoughtfully, and returned his attention to the scenery.

Not far behind the bus, Eric and Edith Bumstead were rattling along at top speed in their stolen hot dog van. As they'd narrowly missed out on their free lunch, they were now hungrier than ever, and had decided that Edith should drive while Eric scoured the cupboards in the back for food. Unfortunately everything that hadn't already fallen out of the flap was uncooked or unrecognizable. Eric had never seen a tortilla before in his life. He assumed they were some sort of cardboard packaging and threw them out on to the road as well.

"What have we got, then?" shouted Edith, hunched over the steering wheel, concentrating on avoiding the huge potholes in the road.

"Sausages, by the look of it," replied Eric. "And some sort of spicy red stuff. Dunno what it is, but it smells funny."

Cooking sausages in a moving vehicle is not a particularly easy or sensible thing to attempt, even on the smoothest of roads, but Eric was determined to give it a go. However, just standing up was proving difficult, as the van lurched and dipped without warning, throwing him against the gas cooker and into piles of saucepans. His mother's little stomach problem hadn't got any better either, and was making him a bit dubious about striking a match to light the gas.

"Are you supposed to fry these things or boil them?" he shouted, never having done either before.

Edith risked a quick glance over her shoulder at the nasty pink thing her son was dangling from his dirty fingers.

"How should I know?" she shrugged. "What does it say on the packet?"

"Er, wait a minute," said Eric, fumbling with a large plastic bag. "Oh, that's no help at all! It's all written in foreign, isn't it! I'll just have to guess."

"You're useless, you are! Get up here and drive! I'll do the food!" shouted Edith, but Eric was determined to manage on his own. Ignoring his mother's continual criticisms and occasional waft of foul-smelling air, he selected a big iron pot, threw a handful of the hot dog sausages into it and lit the cooker. A slightly worrying burning smell and a lot of smoke filled the back of the van. Edith's opinion of her son's domestic skills wasn't very high and suddenly got even lower.

"What on earth are you cooking them in?" she hollered.

"What do you mean, what am I cooking them in?" bellowed Eric defensively. "A saucepan, of course! What d'you think I'm cooking them in? A bath?"

"No, you idiot! I mean are you using cooking oil or water?"

Not being a particularly experienced chef, it hadn't occurred to Eric to use either.

"Oh, right," he said, and began a frantic search through the cupboards again. "We haven't got any. Must've all fallen out when we borrowed the van . . . but there's a big bottle of vinegar!"

Hurriedly he sloshed about a pint of it into the panful of smouldering sausages and then another pint or so on to his trousers and the floor of the van as they lurched sharply round a bend. There was a loud hissing and spitting noise and even more smoke.

"Get up here and drive! Let me do it!" repeated

Edith, terrified they were about to go up in flames.

"Look, just shut up, will you!" shouted her vinegar-soaked son, who was now rubbing his stinging eyes amid a cloud of black smoke. "It's all under control!"

A few eye-watering minutes later, Eric clambered back into the passenger seat with two platefuls of mushy sausages, which he'd cleverly prepared to be partly burnt to a crisp and partly raw. The boiled vinegar marinade certainly added a bit of flavour, as did the unidentified spicy red sauce he'd sloshed all over them, though it was the sort of flavour that meant they were soon both gasping for a drink of water and felt horribly sick.

Meanwhile, aboard the bus, Fintan was attempting to interest Gribley in yet another game of I Spy with little success. Apart from "B" for *bus* and "T" for *trees*, there hadn't been a lot of variation. Fintan looked around his fellow passengers for inspiration and noticed a strangely familiar face. There was a man sitting right at the back wearing partially melted dark glasses and reading a newspaper. He looked uncannily like the man he'd set alight in Café Gordurosa. The only apparent difference was that this man had a big bushy ginger beard instead of a black one, which, if anything, looked even less convincing. For a moment he considered doing "B" for *beard*, which would definitely have foxed Gribley, but thought better of it.

"Hey, Gribs, look!" he whispered, nudging his seatmate in the ribs with unnecessary force. "It's that bloke again!"

"You mustn't point at people like that, sir. It's considered quite rude."

Fintan stopped pointing and gestured by nodding his head instead. "Look! It's the man from the café! But he's got a new beard this time."

Gribley glanced up briefly. It was definitely the same man and definitely quite a coincidence that they should bump into him again. For a moment Gribley wondered whether the man had followed them, angry about the beard-burning incident, but soon dismissed the idea as silly. After all, there was nothing unusual about encountering a Brazilian man on a Brazilian bus, was there? Especially in Brazil!

"I'm going to go and say hello," said Fintan. Despite Gribley's protestations that he should leave the poor man alone, Fintan unsteadily made his way to the back of the lurching bus. The bearded man, having evidently spotted approaching trouble, buried himself in his newspaper.

"Hello, remember me?" said Fintan chirpily. "From the café? Sorry about the newspaper . . . and the beard and all that! It was an accident, you see, honest it was! Hope that wasn't your best beard, by the way. It was a lot nicer than this one, wasn't it. I'll pay for the damage, if you like?"

The man tried staring out of the window in an attempt to ignore Fintan's incessant wittering. It was then that Fintan noticed the fancy-looking walkie-talkie on the vacant seat next to him.

"Wow, I like your walkie-talkie thing! Can I have a look?" he said, snatching it up anyway. "I used to have a pair of these when I was little. Well, I did till my mum confiscated them. Just because I tuned them to the police frequency and caused a few emergencies . . . and a national manhunt or two! Anyway, this one's great! Really heavy! Got loads of knobs, hasn't it! Looks like an army one or something. . ."

"No, no. Please not to touch!" said the man, attempting to retrieve his property before something unfortunate happened to it. Like fire, for instance.

Fintan stood swaying in the aisle, saluted and put on a silly military-type voice.

"Hello, Colonel?" he said into the walkie-talkie. "Yes, this is General Fedora speaking, sir! My tank squadron is at the ready! Over and out!"

"Look, there he is! Standing right at the back of the bus!" screeched Edith, through a mouthful of half-chewed raw sausage. She pointed wildly. "Blimey! You were right! Do you think he's seen us?"

Eric grabbed his mother's hand and pulled it down. "Well he probably has now, you stupid old woman! Stop pointing at him!"

"What's that he's holding?" she added, peering intently. "It's not a gun, is it?"

Eric, who wouldn't have been at all surprised to find young master Fedora was armed to the teeth, tried to focus on the strange dark object he was waving about.

"Nah, it's not a gun. If anything, it looks more like a bomb to me."

"A bomb?" screeched his horrified mother. "Where would he get a bomb from?"

The road to Correntina's granddaughter's village was long, rough, hilly and gradually increased in altitude. It was also extremely bumpy. At that exact moment the bus hit a particularly big bump, causing Fintan to fall backwards between the seats and launch the walkie-talkie out through the back window. Transfixed with sudden terror, the Bumsteads watched the dark object hurtle towards them and smash right through their windscreen. With the "unexploded bomb" lodged between them in Edith's plate of poorly cooked sausages, they screamed in terror, opened their doors and leapt out on to the road. The driverless old hot dog van wobbled wildly about, then suddenly veered off to the left and plunged into the thick greenery, where it disappeared into a gully. Eric and Edith lay on the road with their hands over their heads, waiting for the explosion – which, when it came, wasn't quite as enormous as they'd thought it would be, but enough to shake the jungle and frighten a lot of birds into the air. The fact that it was caused by the gas bottle under the stove, which Eric had forgotten to turn off, didn't occur to them.

This had been attempted murder!

SIXTEEN

Somewhere above the vast rainforest canopy, Max Wrench was seated comfortably in his executive helicopter. A red light began blinking on his satellite phone. This meant it was an important call! The red channel was reserved for secret communications in "Operation Harvest", which was the name Randall had just invented for his company's vital chocoplum-grabbing mission.

"Wrench here, go ahead," he said importantly over the noise of the helicopter's engine.

It was more bad news from Mission HQ, otherwise known as Randall's office. Apparently the tracking device Gonzalez had cunningly implanted in his walkie-talkie had just gone dead and all communication with him had been lost. Worse still, there were reports of an explosion in the vicinity just as the device had gone off line. It appeared that Agent Gonzalez had been "eliminated". The only good news was that before his tragic death, Gonzalez had somehow managed to plant a second tracking device in the boy's rucksack, which meant they could now monitor his position from a safe distance. Wrench bit his lip in frustration. This kid had some nerve! He'd really stepped over the line this time!

"Give me the coordinates," he barked, "I'm going to follow him myself!"

A few hours later, Fintan had just finished apologizing to the driver for the broken window, and resumed apologizing to the ginger-bearded man for losing his walkie-talkie, when the bus finally came to a halt. They had pulled up outside the village where Correntina's granddaughter, Ana, was supposed to be waiting for them. Several of the passengers, including the sulking bearded man, piled off after them into the rapidly darkening evening and collected their bags from the hold. A grumpy-looking teenage girl with long black hair came to meet them.

"You Fedora?" she asked bluntly. It wasn't a particularly warm welcome, but considering they were complete strangers who were only there to get their hands on the family's treasured secret, it was remarkably polite.

Fintan and Gribley grabbed their assorted luggage and followed her down a red earth path between a mass of dark trees. They arrived at the village just as the sun was setting over the jungle and the night's insect population was beginning their almighty chorus.

There weren't many buildings in the village at all, so far as they could see, just a handful of wooden shacks with corrugated iron roofs and very basic facilities. There were a few bushes and banana trees, but otherwise the village stood in an empty clearing of hard, bare earth, marked out with collapsing fences.

"Tonight you stay with my family," said Ana, leading them into a small concrete-walled construction. "We eat. We sleep. Tomorrow I take you to river."

"OK, thanks a lot, then," said Fintan, who – despite the obvious hospitality he was being shown – didn't feel he was all that welcome. He turned to Gribley, raised his eyebrows and made a sort of "Oh dear, what have we let ourselves in for!" face.

Ana's parents were sitting in the corner, stirring something in a metal pot. They gestured for their guests to join them. Fintan looked around for a chair, but as there didn't seem to be one, sat cross-legged on the floor instead.

"Fintan," he said, pointing at himself, then added, "Gribley," and pointed at him too.

Their hosts nodded but apparently didn't speak any English at all. Bowls of something dark brown and steaming were handed around, which Fintan peered at with obvious distaste. Whatever it was, it had stringy lumps and something that looked like kidney beans.

"Yum," he said, and attempted to look delighted.

Ana pointed at the food. "*Feijoada*," she explained. "Meat stew."

Everyone seemed to be waiting for their guests to start eating first, so Gribley took a small, polite spoonful and appeared to enjoy it. Unfortunately, when it came to his food, Fintan was rather less adventurous.

"I don't suppose you've got any peanut butter,

have you?" he asked hopefully, and was immediately poked hard in the ribs by Gribley.

"Eat the meal, sir," he hissed. "It's very impolite not to, and these people have cooked it especially for us!"

As it turned out, the food wasn't bad at all, and neither were the woven mats they were offered to sleep on afterwards. With the addition of a comfy sleeping bag and an inflatable pillow, Fintan happily settled down for a good night's sleep. In fact, compared to the catering and accommodation currently being enjoyed by the unfortunate Gonzalez, they were living in genuine luxury. Outside in the dark, the poor man sat beneath a tree, peeled off his itchy ginger beard and ate a few broken biscuits he'd brought along. With nothing else to do, he curled up under his coat and tried to get comfortable.

The ground was hard, lumpy and a bit damp, and the air was full of little biting insects. Even more irritating, though, were the half-dozen or so scrawny village dogs that wouldn't leave him alone and periodically came and peed on his head. By the time dawn broke, he was feeling considerably less bright and breezy than the inhabitants of the nearby little concrete building. He smelled a lot worse too.

"Morning, Gribs!" said Fintan cheerily. "Today's the day we hit the jungle! Exciting, eh?"

Gribley opened his eyes and steeled himself for another day of danger and discomfort. The whole household was up quickly, and they quietly set about preparing a kind of thick, stodgy porridge to see them on their way. Fintan, who was finally learning some manners, ate without complaint and thanked the family for their kindness.

Within half an hour they were ready to go, and emerged from the hut weighed down with their gear. Ana looked critically at the two improbable-looking explorers who were already staggering beneath their huge rucksacks, hip bags, bum bags and bed rolls, as well as sundry pots and containers tied on with string.

"Why you bring so much stuff?" she said. "Too heavy for forest. You mad boy!"

"No, I'm not!" insisted Fintan. "This is all very important explorer's equipment! I haven't packed anything I don't need!"

Ana didn't look convinced.

"Why you need these?" she asked disapprovingly, gesturing towards his collection of plastic boxes.

"They're dual function!" said Fintan, thinking it sounded highly technical. "They've got sandwiches in, and then when they're empty they'll be perfect for keeping the fruit samples in. And anyway, they're really light!"

"Why you bring big iron cooking pot, then? Very heavy!"

Fintan tutted, as if this was completely obvious. "Because it's another dual function item, of course! *Young Adventurer* magazine says that iron pots with lids are good for keeping things safe in . . . and for cooking in too!"

He decided not to mention the fact that it was also currently stuffed full of peanut butter sandwiches.

"Too much stuff. Too heavy for forest," repeated Ana, apparently unswayed by Fintan's explanations. He frowned, rapidly beginning to dislike his young guide. She reminded him a bit too much of his older sister, who thought she knew best, didn't give him any credit at all and was constantly finding something to criticize. He hadn't come halfway across the world to put up with the same nonsense he could get at home, so it was with some relief that he realized Ana didn't intend to accompany them for the whole journey.

After a fairly gruelling two-hour hike along some tricky forest paths, they came to a halt at a fast-flowing brown river.

"I stop here," announced Ana, and promptly sat down on the ground. Gribley and Fintan took off their heavy packs and gratefully slumped down after her. A quick glance convinced Fintan that there were no chocoplum trees in the vicinity, which meant they weren't actually there yet.

"Now what?" he asked.

Ana produced a crumpled sheet of paper from her small bag, on which she'd written directions and drawn a rough map. Before handing it over, she hesitated and fixed both her guests with a serious gaze.

"You make promise to my grandmother not to harm trees. . ." she said earnestly. "Now you promise me too. You promise me you never tell where you found them and you never return. OK? One day my grandchildren want fruits too."

Fintan and Gribley, conscious of her very serious expression and tone of voice, nodded their heads solemnly.

"We promise," they said.

"Cross my heart and hope t—" began Fintan, before realizing it probably wasn't appropriate.

Ana handed Gribley the map, as he appeared to be the more trustworthy of the two, then got up and began uncovering a shallow boat which had been concealed with branches.

"You bring boat back too!" she added, with another stern gaze.

Lurking behind a nearby cluster of trees which hung heavy with moss and ancient vines, Gonzalez was watching all this with great interest. Despite the fact that his only means of communicating with HQ had been destroyed, he had been instructed to follow the boy, and that was exactly what he was going to continue to do. What's more, he was going to do it extremely warily, from a safe distance, and was determined not to be fooled by Fedora's "idiot boy" act again. He looked through his binoculars and confirmed that the girl had indeed given them a map, presumably to the valley where they'd find the fruit grove. This was excellent! He swatted away the irritating cloud of little flies which billowed around his head, attracted by the smell of dog wee, and made a mental note to wash himself in the river at his earliest opportunity.

SEVENTEEN

Somewhere near the top of a massive New York office building, an entire floor was buzzing with excitement and activity. It wasn't often that Randall T. Buckmeister called an urgent meeting of all his top executives, advertising and marketing people ... but that was exactly what he had just done, and at very short notice too. Obviously something important was happening! Hordes of smartly suited young businesspeople with briefcases crowded out of the lift and converged on Giganti-Foods International's impressively huge boardroom.

Randall himself was already seated at the head of a massive polished oak table, sifting through a stack of papers. The executives took their seats, switched their mobiles to silent and opened their laptops. Whatever this was, it was obviously big.

Eventually, the great Mr Buckmeister stopped arranging his notes and cleared his throat.

"Ladies and gentlemen of the board," he announced, "this is big."

Assorted little murmurings of "I told you it was big" ran excitedly around the table.

"We at Giganti-Foods International pride ourselves on being the biggest and the best in the world... And I've called you here today to tell you that, believe it or not, we're about to get even bigger! We are about to become the sole possessors of the world's rarest and most delicious fruit..." He paused for dramatic effect. "The legendary chocoplum!"

Another little wave of muttering rippled through the assembled employees, ranging from gasps of awe to mumbled disbelief. Their boss had gone insane!

"This is a fruit so exotic that most people think it's just a myth. But we at Giganti-Foods aren't easily discouraged. Not even by things that don't exist! We are visionaries! We are prepared to look beyond that myth and make it a reality! At this very moment, deep in the Brazilian rainforest, I have a crack team on the verge of possessing our prize! I have mobilized our vast resources to ensure that this mission is a complete success, and believe me, this is no minor operation! We have flown in the world's most sophisticated computer tracking equipment. We have forest-clearing machinery to make a landing pad, and we have armed men to protect our property in case any of our competitors try to steal it from us. Furthermore, we have a fleet of the world's most advanced cargo helicopters ready to refrigerate the entire crop of these fruits and transport them back to our processing plants."

Amid yet more gasps and mumbling, one senior executive felt moved to ask a question, and raised his hand.

"Er, excuse me, Mr Buckmeister, sir," he said with understandable hesitation, "but did you say we're taking the entire crop? Is that really necessary?"

Randall lowered his glasses and stared hard at the poor unfortunate questioner.

"What's your name, son?" he asked.

"Binkmeyer, sir."

"Well, Binkmeyer," he continued, coldly, "in

answer to your question . . . of course it's necessary, you idiot! These fruits ONLY grow in this one place in the entire world! If we leave any trees behind, what's going to happen? Someone else is going to take them, that's what! Meaning we won't be the ONLY company marketing them! Understand?"

Thoroughly chastised, Binkmeyer hung his head in shame, convinced he'd just ruined any chance of promotion.

"This is a serious business! We are not playing around here! These rare delicacies are going to be OURS and ours alone! We will leave nothing behind. Nothing! Not a single tree stump, branch or seed!"

The boardroom fell completely silent. They were a group of highly experienced, hardened executives, familiar with the cut-throat nature of big business practice, but this was extraordinary stuff. It was greedy, selfish, unethical and probably highly illegal too, but no one dared say a word.

Randall checked his notes and began his conclusion.

"Pretty soon I'm going to be speaking to the press. First up, a teaser campaign. We tell them something big's coming but we don't tell them what. We start a buzz. We get them speculating. We maximize the publicity. Now then, I want all you people to get on to this campaign, top priority, and I want it to be massive. So ... get to work! Give it all you've got and I promise you all one thing right now: this is going to make me – I mean make us – an absolute fortune!"

EIGHTEEN

Gonzalez was hiding in the undergrowth peering through his binoculars and trying hard to suppress a fit of giggles. For several minutes he'd been watching the hilarious spectacle of Fintan attempting to learn how to paddle a wooden canoe. The older man sitting at the front had mastered the paddling technique fairly quickly but was being seriously let down by the gangly idiot sitting at the back. Despite Ana's shouted instructions from the bank, they could do nothing more than wobble from one side of the river to the other, where they'd wedge in the mud and occasionally go round in circles.

When it eventually became clear which direction they were supposed to be heading in, Gonzalez crept furtively downstream through the trees to survey the land ahead. It seemed he would have no problem trailing them on foot, which was lucky, as there was no sign of a second boat anywhere. He could see through his binoculars, however, that a short distance ahead, the river split into two. That wasn't good. If they took the right fork, he would be stuck on the wrong side of the river and lose them. He ran a little way upstream and considered his options. There didn't appear to be many. Several massive jungle trees overhung the water, and one in particular looked like a pretty good way to get across to the other side. He swatted the annoying flies away from his smelly hair, climbed carefully up the tree and began crawling out along a large, leafy branch.

A short distance back downriver, Ana had finally managed to explain to Fintan where he was going wrong. With their canoe pointing roughly in the right direction, the strong current took hold of them and they were away. Hurriedly, they shouted their thanks and waved farewells to their guide. Fintan was pretty certain he wouldn't miss her, but Gribley wasn't so sure. He was about to head deep into the

Amazon rainforest with an accident-prone fourteen-year-old boy who couldn't even paddle in a straight line. This was an extremely worrying prospect, and one he couldn't believe he had allowed himself to be talked into.

Gonzalez crawled into position on his branch, took cover behind a mass of leaves and lifted his binoculars to his eyes. He could hear them coming before he could actually see them. Fintan was sloshing his long wooden paddle around with all the grace of an ice-skating giraffe. Gribley was trying to get him to paddle in rhythm but it seemed the boy had no sense of timing at all. Most of his attempts resulted in him swiping the surrounding bushes or sticking his oar in the mud. Even when he did manage to get the right end of it in the water, it only resulted in a lot a splashing and very little forward momentum.

"The river forks here, sir," said Gribley, ignoring the waves of dirty brown water Fintan was sloshing on to the back of his head. "According to Ana's map, we need to go to the right, so you'll need to paddle on your right side so we steer that way."

"OK," said Fintan, plunging his oar in on his

left side.

Gonzalez tutted to himself from behind his clump of leaves. Perhaps the boy really was an idiot! The fact that they were heading to the right did mean, however, that he had been right to plan ahead, as he would now have to climb to the opposite bank to avoid losing them.

"No, sir, paddle on the OTHER side!" shouted Gribley, wondering why they were heading towards the wrong fork. "The other side!"

"Oh, sorry, Gribs," said Fintan, quickly hoisting his oar overhead in a huge swinging arc.

The mathematical odds against hitting a man in the face with an eight-foot paddle while he is hiding in a tree in the jungle are astronomically huge. However, that was exactly what happened. Gonzalez was vaguely aware of a hard, flat object suddenly appearing before his eyes and hearing a loud cracking sound before fading into unconsciousness. He slumped senseless on to his branch, then slowly slid out of the tree and into the river.

Fintan and Gribley didn't hear the loud splash made by Gonzalez hitting the water behind them, as it was masked by all the other loud splashes coming from the back end of the boat. After a lot of effort and precarious wobbling about, they managed to persuade their shallow wooden canoe to go the right way.

Gonzalez wasn't unconscious for very long. In fact, as soon as the first sudden rush of muddy water forced itself up his nose, he rapidly recovered some of his senses. His eyes flew open and stared in shock. It appeared the world had got a lot thicker. It had also turned a murky shade of greeny brown and had lumps floating in it. This, and the fact that he was finding it difficult to breathe, suggested he was drowning. Gasping and retching, he clawed his way up to the surface and flailed uselessly around before grabbing at a floating branch. Breathing heavily, he clung to his moss-covered life raft and grew increasingly furious. He could scarcely believe it, but Fintan had outwitted him yet again! The idiot kid had somehow got the better of him for a third time!

On the plus side, however, he wasn't dead, and he could still hear Fintan's hopeless attempts at paddling, which meant his enemy couldn't be far ahead. He also didn't have to worry about smelling of dog wee any more. For a moment he contemplated getting back on to the bank, but as the strong river current was carrying him along behind them, he decided he might as well stay in the water and let the current do the work. After a while, a slightly sturdier raft of jungle foliage floated alongside him, which would offer better camouflage. Cunningly concealed by leaves and clutching the slippery moss-covered log, Gonzalez drifted discreetly along behind, keeping a watchful eye on Fintan up ahead.

This wasn't so bad, he told himself. Certainly a lot easier than walking! This positive thought managed to keep him cheerful for a while. Well, it did until he entered the bit of the river with the piranhas in it.

NINETEEN

After spending several unhappy hours sitting on the roadside arguing about what to do next, and whose fault it was that they had to do it, the Bumsteads had managed to flag down a passing lorry. Encountering any traffic at all along the isolated forest road was extremely rare, so they were grateful to have a lift. They sat in the cab of the huge logging truck laden with enormous tree trunks and grinned at the driver. He appeared to speak no English at all, which suited them perfectly, as they were no good at polite conversation and hadn't yet thought up a reasonable explanation as to how they'd got there. The driver was just as happy to ignore his passengers, though he did wind down his window fairly quickly to get some fresh air. Tinny music played non-stop on the man's radio, which was turned up far too loud.

After an hour or so of uneventful lurching and bumping along amid endless dense forest, the music stopped for a news bulletin. Eric and Edith of course had no idea what the Brazilian newsreader was saying, but did notice that the truck driver suddenly started looking at them in a funny way. As indeed he would. According to the radio news, a fat young man and skinny old woman of European appearance had viciously attacked an innocent hot dog vendor in Santos Coelho and stolen his vehicle. Police were warning the public not to approach them, as they were considered highly dangerous. Armed units were at that moment searching for the fugitives and their stolen vehicle and had set up road blocks to catch them. Aware that the trucker was eyeing him suspiciously, Eric grinned stupidly and made a matey thumbs-up gesture. It didn't appear to make the driver any more friendly.

The tinny music returned and the truck rumbled on. For another hour or so, no one spoke. Eric and Edith gazed vacantly out of the window at the seemingly endless forest while the truck driver gave them the odd dirty look. Eventually, the lorry began to slow as they entered a small dilapidated-looking town. It wasn't much of a town. Just a meagre cluster of houses, a petrol station and something that appeared to be a general store. Ahead there was a short line of stationary traffic.

"Typical," tutted Edith. "Miles from nowhere and we get stuck in a traffic jam!"

Eric craned his neck to see what was causing the hold-up. About a hundred yards ahead was a line of police cars with their blue lights flashing and several policemen searching the passing vehicles. This wasn't good! The police made Eric nervous, mostly because they tended to arrest him quite a lot. It then occurred to him that he had recently stolen a hot dog van in broad daylight in front of dozens of witnesses. This definitely wasn't good!

"We'd better get out of here," he said urgently to his mother, who was contentedly humming along with a tune on the radio.

"What?" she said. "Why? This isn't a proper town. This is the middle of nowhere! What are we gonna do here?"

Eric gestured as subtly as possible towards the

blue flashing lights. "There's a police road block – look! I reckon they're after us."

Edith still had a bit of catching up to do.

"Don't be daft. Why would they be after us? We didn't do nothing! It was the Fedora kid what blew up the va. . ." A five-watt bulb of understanding lit a dark corner of her gloomy mind. "Oh, right. We nicked the van!" she said.

The driver changed down another gear, and, keeping a suspicious eye on his passengers, brought the truck to a halt with a loud hissing of brakes. Eric immediately grabbed the door handle and grinned at the driver again.

"We'll get out here, mate," he said quickly. "Cheers for the lift, an' all that!"

The pair of scruffy fugitives scrambled down from the lorry's cab and began walking briskly towards its rear end, where they could take cover.

"Now what do we do?" muttered Edith, preparing herself for another round of criticizing her useless son.

"I dunno, do I!" blurted Eric. "Gimme a chance!"

On the left of the road was the same impenetrable

mass of rainforest they'd been passing through for hours. On the right was the little general store.

"Come on, we can go in there," said Eric, and quickly scuttled over to it. Edith followed behind, deliberately looking anywhere but towards the waiting police cars. The store was, as might be expected, virtually empty. In a remote community like this, there weren't many regular customers, so it catered to passing trade like loggers and truck drivers. Unfortunately it also seemed to cater for the occasional heavily armed police patrol. In fact, apart from Eric and Edith, the only other person browsing in the shop was a huge, mean-looking policeman with a dark moustache, dark glasses and a gun hanging from his belt.

"Act natural, stay calm. . ." whispered Eric to his terrified-looking mother, then picked up a basket and pretended to be looking at the shelves. Edith followed his example and grabbed a basket of her own. The only problem with this ploy was that they were both painfully hungry again and the shelves were packed with a tempting array of food. Edith's stomach churned noisily, still attempting to digest a mixture of semi-poisonous berries and semicooked sausages. Not wishing to attract unwanted attention, she bit her lip and forced herself to keep her smelly convulsions inside for once. Eric strolled down an aisle full of family-sized bags of crisps and nuts and tried to think rationally. It looked likely that they'd have to make a run for it any minute, so he might as well pick up a few essentials while he could. Seeing as they were already wanted for vehicle theft and assault, a little bit of shoplifting couldn't make things much worse.

Having decided on his idiotic plan of action, he immediately began stuffing as much junk as he could into his basket ... crisps, biscuits, beer, sweets, cake and some funny-looking things covered in pastry. Edith, noticing her son's sudden shoplifting spree, realized what he was up to and started to grab large handfuls of items herself. They were just shovelling an entire display of chocolate biscuits into their baskets when the shop door opened behind them.

It was the logging truck driver again, only this time he wasn't alone. He appeared to have found an even bigger armed policeman than the one who was already there. Eric and the huge Brazilian policeman made eye contact, and for a moment stood dead still.

Realizing it was now or never, the Bumsteads let out a shriek, barged past them and ran straight out of the open door. There was a sudden barrage of angry Portuguese shouting behind them, which they assumed meant something like "Yes, that's them, officer!" and "Stop or I shoot!" Without waiting to find out, they belted as fast as they could across the road. Further warnings were shouted and ignored, closely followed by cracks of gunfire. Still clutching their heavily laden shopping baskets, Eric and Edith hollered in mortal terror and plunged into the thick tropical undergrowth.

"Now what do we do?" screeched Edith, not used to being shot at.

"Just keep running!" advised her son, who wasn't used to being shot at either but was pretty familiar with running away. The angry shouts grew louder. It appeared several other policemen had joined their colleagues and were giving chase, firing as they went. More bullets zipped past their heads and thudded into the trees. Not being particularly athletic, it was pure undiluted fear that enabled the

Bumsteads to run full tilt into the jungle. For more than twenty minutes they weaved through the dense maze of greenery and didn't even stop when a couple of packets of chocolate biscuits fell out of Edith's basket.

"Eric!" Edith wheezed eventually. "Eric, stop! I can't run any more!"

Red-faced and sweating profusely, they stopped and slumped to the ground. Apart from the noise of a few insects and their own unhealthy, gasping breath, the forest was completely quiet. Several minutes passed with no sound of gunfire or shouts from pursuing policemen. It looked like they had lost them. Unfortunately it also seemed they had lost themselves. One bit of rainforest looked very much like any other bit. They had no map, no compass, no survival gear, no tents, hammocks or sleeping bags. Worse still, they had no idea where they were or what they were going to do next.

They did, however, have some edible food for a change. As soon as they'd got their breathing under control, they helped themselves to several bags of crisps each, opened some cans of beer and cheered themselves up with a long-overdue picnic.

TWENTY

By the time they'd covered their first five miles of river, Fintan's paddling had improved considerably. He was hitting the back of Gribley's head with his oar a lot less often. Progress had been erratic and at times frightening, but somehow, with the help of the current, they had stayed on course and not got lost at all. Daylight was fading fast and Fintan was fading even faster. Ironically, just as he actually seemed to have got the hang of paddling, they reached the landmark Ana had told them to look out for, and had to stop.

On their left-hand side was a steep bank of pinkish rock split by a spectacular waterfall, where a separate river tributary flowed into theirs. Ana had made it very clear that they should abandon the boat here before the two rivers merged, and to keep well clear of the resulting dangerous waters. Luckily Gribley had remembered this important piece of information and steered them to the right side, where they managed to drag the boat up the shallow muddy bank.

Unused to such hard physical work, they hauled their heavy packs from the boat and set up their first proper jungle camp with aching arms. Rather than a tent, they had brought hammocks which could be suspended between trees and covered with mosquito nets. Once these were ready, they sat exhausted on an old mossy log and planned their evening meal. This meant gathering dry wood for a fire and finding a temporary home for the peanut butter sandwich collection so they could use the cooking pot. Gribley, being well skilled in the culinary arts, was able to produce a surprisingly good stew from the dried ingredients he'd brought along, and the cup of hot tea he made next was the best thing they'd tasted in days!

After a quick clean-up, Fintan restocked and sealed the pot, then produced a length of rope from his rucksack. Gribley watched, intrigued, as he threw the rope over a tree branch, tied one end to the handle of the iron cooking pot and began hauling it several feet into the air.

"May I ask what you're doing, Master Fintan?" enquired Gribley.

Fintan grinned, proud of his advanced jungle survival knowledge.

"Ah! It's something I read about in *Young Adventurer*," he said. "All the famous jungle explorers do this. You're supposed to hang your food up a tree so that animals can't get to it."

"I'm fairly sure they couldn't get to it anyway, sir," observed Gribley. "It is secured inside a strong iron pot with a fixed lid, after all."

"Can't be too sure, though! Some of these animals are pretty clever!" said Fintan, sagely, while attempting to tie the end of the rope to a tree trunk.

"Please be sure to tie a strong knot, sir. We wouldn't want it to fall, would we."

Fintan tutted at Gribley's obvious lack of faith in his practical ability.

"Duh! Of course I will!" he said dismissively. "I used to be in the Cub Scouts, remember?"

"Indeed, sir," said Gribley. "Though if I remember correctly, it was a rather brief membership. They were a little upset about that scout hut burning down."

"Relax, Gribs! If there's one thing I'm good at, it's tying secure knots!" said Fintan with an air of finality. Unfortunately his left bootlace was undone and trailing in the mud as he said it.

By now it was completely dark and they were thoroughly worn out. There seemed little left to do but climb into their hammocks and go to sleep.

A few hours later dawn broke over the jungle. About half a mile west of Fintan's camp, Wrench's black executive helicopter was hovering noisily above the canopy, thrashing the treetops with the downblast from its rotors. According to his data, they were directly over the map coordinates of his planned dropping point. The rainforest was, of course, far too dense to allow a landing, so he was carefully winched down to the forest floor, followed by his rucksack full of fantastically expensive technical equipment. Once safely on the ground, he signalled for the pilot to depart and immediately checked his tracking gear. A little red light was blinking on and off and making a satisfying "beep" noise. The tiny device Gonzalez had planted in Fintan's rucksack appeared to be working perfectly, and indicating that young master Fedora was, as expected, very close by. So close by, in fact, that his nice lie-in had been ruined.

"Did you hear that, Gribs?" he said from the depths of his sleeping bag. "Sounded like a helicopter!"

"Indeed I did, sir," replied Gribley, who was already up and preparing breakfast. "Rather unusual to hear one this deep into the rainforest, I imagine."

After a good bowl of porridge and a nice mug of tea, Gribley and Fintan dismantled their camp and packed their damp, sweaty gear into their rucksacks. It was only an hour or so after dawn and already stiflingly hot, so they made sure they had plenty of drinking water handy. Gribley had, of course, had the sense to bring a compass, so after consulting Ana's map, he was able to work out roughly which direction to walk in.

"When's it going to be my turn to have the map?" asked Fintan eagerly. "I want to be group leader today, please!"

Reluctantly, Gribley handed over the vital scrap of paper, but kept the compass and made a mental note to be involved in any navigation decisions. With their heavy loads hoisted on to their backs, they set off into the thick tangle of jungle.

A few hundred yards away, Wrench noticed the little red light begin to move on his tracking screen. Things were going perfectly to plan! The idiot boy was going to lead him straight to the legendary chocoplum grove! Quickly he grabbed his super lightweight, high-tech equipment and followed from a safe distance.

Walking through rainforest terrain isn't easy. The ground underfoot is uneven, strewn with fallen branches and roots that can trip the unwary. It can quickly change from slippery leaf cover to squelchy ankle-deep mud. It involves struggling up steep, treacherous slopes and slithering down rocky gullies. As if this isn't bad enough, the trees can be covered in nasty sharp spikes and an assortment of vicious, poisonous leaves. There are things crawling around in the trees, too, which are only too happy to bite, nibble and sting any warm-blooded creature that walks by. There are snakes and mosquitoes and scorpions and leeches and even the possibility of the odd hungry jaguar. On top of all this, though, is the heat. A dull, heavy, energy-sapping, humid heat that sits on you and weighs you down like a soggy duvet.

"Don't forget to keep drinking your water, sir. You mustn't get dehydrated," said Gribley at regular intervals during the day, prompted by Fintan's prolonged bouts of silence and occasional stumble.

"I'm fine, thanks," insisted Fintan, despite feeling thoroughly exhausted. "Can we just stop here a minute, though, and have another look at the map?"

It was the third time they'd stopped and checked the map in the last two hours, and each time there had been a disagreement followed by a change of direction. This time didn't look any different.

"Actually, Gribs, I reckon you were right last time . . . we should've gone left, not straight on," said Fintan, still a little confused as to how the compass worked. "Sorry about that. You probably shouldn't listen to my suggestions. I'm usually wrong!"

Ever patient and tolerant, Gribley resisted the urge to say "I told you so" but agreed that they should turn around, retrace their path and then follow the new course.

Staring at his bleeping device, Wrench noted this new change of direction with alarm. The chaotic zigzagging route they'd been taking could mean only one thing. They must have worked out they were being followed and were trying to shake him off! Cursing this bit of bad luck, he turned to follow them, and shrieked in terror as he came face to face with a wild-looking apparition. There was a tall, dark man with incredibly messy, matted hair staring directly at him. His face was scratched and blotchy and covered in what looked like little teeth marks. Weirder still, he was wearing a pair of half-melted sunglasses and had the tufty remains of a false ginger beard glued to his face in little patches.

Wrench fumbled for his gun and pointed it shakily at the terrifying wild man.

"Stay back!" he stammered, his voice squeaky with fear. "I'm armed, see!"

Much to his surprise, the man began pointing at

the Giganti-Foods International logo emblazoned across Wrench's jacket.

"Don't shoot!" he said with a strong Brazilian accent. "I'm on your side!"

He reached into his ragged trouser pocket, produced a Giganti-Foods International identity card and held it up for inspection.

"Gonzalez?" said Wrench, when he'd recovered from the sudden shock. The wreck of a man nodded. "But I thought you were dead!"

For the next few minutes Gonzalez explained his long, unfortunate story, right up to the point where he'd been swept into the dangerous waters beneath the waterfall and pummelled around like a load of washing on spin cycle. It had been a painful battering, but had at least shaken off the last of the piranhas. He was also able to report the good news that Fintan didn't appear to be armed. However, it was the news that the boy was in possession of a map that Wrench found most exciting.

"What?" he exclaimed. "A map? To the fruit trees? And no gun? Why didn't you say so before?"

Gonzalez shrugged, "How could I?" he said "He threw my walkie-talkie out of the bus!"

This was fantastic news for Wrench. It meant he didn't have to trudge around following in the idiot kid's meandering footsteps any more! All he had to do was walk straight up to him and take the map! An image of taking candy from a baby popped into his head. The rules of the game had just changed in his favour!

TWENTY-ONE

Darkness falls quickly in the jungle. Fintan and Gribley hadn't gone much further when they were forced to stop and prepare for their second night in the wild. They tied their hammocks again, built a small fire and ate another stew. Exhausted by the day's endeavours, they were ready to sleep soon after. Fintan hoisted their food supplies aloft again, tied another wobbly knot and changed into his special jungle pyjamas, which he'd chosen because they had little pictures of explorers in pith helmets all over them.

"Sleep well, sir," said Gribley, having carefully removed a few nasty-looking bugs from his sleeping bag.

"G'night, Gribs," replied Fintan. There was a

short pause before he decided this might be a good time to get something off his chest. "Actually, I've been thinking. . ." he said.

"Really, sir?" replied Gribley, unused to this sort of thing. "What about?"

"About you calling me 'sir' all the time, Gribs. I mean, we're not at home now, are we? We're miles from home in the middle of nowhere! You shouldn't have to call me sir here, should you?"

Gribley was surprised. It was such a habit that he didn't even realize he was doing it.

"Er, I hadn't realized it might be an issue, sir," he said, demonstrating his point.

"You must know what I mean, though?" added Fintan. "We're on an expedition together! We're fellow explorers! Can't we just talk to each other like, you know, 'mates' or something while we're out here?"

"Well, I shall try, of course, if that's what you wish. . ." said Gribley, making a conscious effort not to add "sir". "But I think I might find that a little difficult to maintain. You must bear in mind that we are not actually 'friends' at all. I am an employee of your family, and am here in that capacity.

Remember, your father is paying me to escort you on this journey."

Even though this was all quite true, Gribley felt he was perhaps being a little unfair. Their relationship wasn't one of friends or equals as such, but they had known each other for years and there was definitely an element of friendship between them. The boy meant well. It wasn't his fault he was such a disaster!

"Hmm . . . s'pose so," said Fintan, sounding a bit hurt and disappointed.

Gribley, feeling a bit guilty, was just about to concede that he would definitely try to cut down on the "sir" front, when he was distracted by something crawling along his arm. He leapt up within the narrow confines of his mosquito net and brushed something scaly off into the darkness.

"What was that?" said Fintan, switching on his head torch in alarm.

"I'm not sure, sir – er . . . I mean, master Fintan . . . possibly a scorpion." Gribley also found his torch and searched around in his hammock for the intruder, randomly smacking at things with a shoe.

Still a little upset by their conversation, Fintan

144

decided he didn't approve of this callous behaviour.

"There's no need to kill it, Gribs!" he protested sulkily. "Leave the poor thing alone!"

"But they carry quite an unpleasant sting!" stammered Gribley, amazed at Fintan's sudden conversion to animal rights.

"Yeah, but that doesn't mean you have to kill it, does it!" said Fintan, climbing down from his hammock. "It's just looking for somewhere cosy to sleep, same as you and me! Give it to me, Gribs, and I'll put it somewhere safe."

Still not convinced by this sudden concern for all the forest's "poor innocent things", Gribley conducted a thorough, but slightly less violent, search of his sleeping area. It was indeed a scorpion. A really big one too, and it wasn't alone. It appeared he'd been sharing his sleeping bag with a whole family of them, and a pair of big, black, hairy tarantulas, who had joined them for good measure.

"Poor things!" said Fintan without much obvious conviction. "Come here, I won't let the mean man hurt you!"

Having wrapped the "poor little innocent creatures" in a vest, he pottered away into the trees.

"Master Fintan, sir!" called Gribley. "It's very unwise to leave the camp in the dark, sir! You might get lost!"

"Oh, stop worrying, will you!" replied Fintan crossly. "I've got my head torch on and I'm not going far!"

Amazingly, he was back within a couple of minutes, without his poisonous little friends, and without having got lost, been attacked by something or fallen into something nasty.

"Right," he announced, climbing back into his hammock and sleeping bag, "maybe now we can get some kip!"

Gribley agreed and wished him goodnight again. He knew Fintan wouldn't be sulking for long. He never did. And even if Gribley was a family employee, he would also make more of an effort not to call Fintan "sir" quite so often. As jobs went, this wasn't a bad one. If anything, it was a surprisingly strange and occasionally exciting one. And he had to admit that although life with Fintan was unpredictable, perilous and chaotic, this was certainly never dull!

"Just out of interest," said Gribley, "did you find

somewhere to put the creatures?"

"I did!" announced Fintan proudly. "I hadn't gone all that far and I found a pair of old boots lying on the ground, so I put them inside. Bit of luck, eh!"

First thing the following morning, they were both shocked awake by a blood-curdling scream which echoed through the forest. It sounded really close by, too. It seemed remarkably unlikely, out here in the middle of nowhere, but Gribley couldn't help wondering whether those old boots had belonged to someone after all.

TWENTY-TWO

When Wrench had finished emptying the stinging menagerie from his boots and applying plasters to his ravaged feet, he double-checked the little beeps coming out of his tracking device and grinned vengefully. If the beeps were to be trusted, then it meant Fintan was less than fifty yards away and he wasn't moving. On the other hand, it could mean that Fintan had found the device planted in his rucksack and thrown it into the bushes to lead them in the wrong direction. If he was as cunning and ruthless as they thought, then it was more likely to be the latter. Either way, the sooner they found out, the better.

"OK, Gonzalez," said Wrench, handing him one of his many spare guns, "here's the plan! We split up and approach the kid's camp as quietly as possible from two different directions. You take the north and I'll come in from the west. We're armed, and we're pretty sure he's not, so taking the map should be simple!"

Gonzalez nodded, grinned and gave a thumbs up sign, then moved off into the trees, brandishing his revolver. If the kid put up any resistance or tried to make a run for it he'd have no hesitation in pulling the trigger, and would probably enjoy it too. Wrench turned the tracker's beeping volume down to minimum, checked his gun was fully loaded and tentatively began his approach.

Meanwhile, several hundred yards to the east of Fintan's camp, Eric and Edith Bumstead were making their slightly less stealthy way through the thick forest. Their supply of crisps and beer had long since disappeared and they hadn't yet managed to find another shop where they could restock. They had come to the painful realization that wearing their old trainers and ill-fitting air hostess uniforms wasn't ideal for jungle exploration. Their feet were so soggy and blistered they could barely walk, and it smelled like something had died inside their socks. With their sleeves and trouser legs ripped by thorns and stained by a variety of unpleasant things, the pair of them looked as if they had been lost for months rather than days. The conversation, however, was pretty much the same as it had always been.

"Why I ever let you talk me into this, I'll never know!" Edith was moaning. "You drag me halfway round the world on your stupid wild goose chase and get me lost in a horrible sweaty jungle! You do realize that if I die here it'll be all your fault, don't you?"

Eric didn't answer, but ground his teeth and stumbled clumsily onwards. In fact, he hadn't answered for an hour or so now, in the hope that his mother might run out of unpleasant things to say and shut up. It wasn't working.

"How did I ever manage to give birth to such an idiot son?" she went on. "Other people's sons don't make their mothers crawl around in dangerous places like this with nothing to eat! They bring them nice cups of tea and biscuits and say 'Would you like another cushion, Mum?'

and 'Shall I put your telly programme on for you, Mum?'... Not you, though. Oh no! No fear of that from my son! Nothing but trouble, that's all you've ever b—"

"Shhh!" hissed Eric, abruptly stopping in his tracks. "I can see smoke ... I think it's a campfire!"

Edith paused in her rant and looked at where her son was pointing. A sudden cold dread gripped them both. Prior to the conversation about how useless Eric was, they had spent some time frightening each other with rumours of hostile local tribes. They had swapped plenty of ill-informed rumours about wild men, headhunters and gruesome stories about huge tribes of cannibals like the ones they'd seen in terrible films. For some time now they'd both been secretly worrying about the possibility of such an encounter actually being real. Eric had occasionally tried cheering himself up by picturing his charming mother tied up and gagged in a cooking pot, but all of a sudden it didn't seem quite so funny.

"I can hear voices!" said Edith, with a terrified look on her gaunt old face. "Listen!"

They listened. Much to their surprise and

immense relief, the cannibals weren't discussing spear-sharpening techniques but were, amazingly enough, comparing the merits of various types of sandwich. And they were speaking English!

Eric's fat stubbly face lit up.

"Wait, I know that voice!" he said. "It's HIM again!"

This was an unbelievable stroke of luck! They'd wandered hopelessly lost through a huge rainforest with no idea where they were heading and bumped right into the kid whose fault it was they were there in the first place! What were the chances? Mother and son exchanged the first friendly glance they'd managed in days.

"Can you believe this! We've finally got him!" said Eric, adopting a hoarse whisper. "And this time there's no bus for him to get away on!"

Edith bared her nasty teeth in what passed for a smile. At last they were about to get their hands on their quarry, which meant they were about to get their hands on huge piles of his father's money! With any luck the boy would put up a bit of a struggle and they would have an excuse to batter him about a bit too! She picked up a sturdy stick from the forest floor and imagined whacking it down on the boy's head. The nasty smile broadened still further. Eric too armed himself with a big stick and began picturing himself finally getting his revenge on that nasty spoilt little kid!

Unaware of the three-pronged pincer movement which was slowly closing in on him, a much less sulky Fintan sat happily toasting a peanut butter sandwich he'd impaled on a stick. The air was full of the incredible range of noises which filled the jungle morning. The usual army of insects were happily chirping, chirring and clicking unseen in the mass of undergrowth. Dozens of parrots and parakeets squawked and shrieked in the air overhead and a variety of small monkeys chattered and howled in the treetops.

"Noisy place, isn't it, Gribs," Fintan said. "You know, considering it's in the countryside and all that! You'd have thought it'd be a lot quieter than this!" Gribley, who was busy untying his hammock from the nearby trees, agreed.

"A surprisingly noisy environment, as you say, sir. . . And most interesting to observe that some of the sounds made by the primates could almost be mistaken for the cries of humans."

"Can you see him?" hissed Edith to her lump of a son, by now almost within striking distance of their prey.

"Not yet, but I can hear him ... going on about animals or somethin' stupid," Eric whispered back. He suddenly froze, struck by the horrible, clammy feeling that he'd been spotted. Which he had. But not by Fintan or Gribley. Crouching in the bushes just a few paces away was a strange-looking Brazilian man with a gun and an expression of surprise.

"Mum," said Eric through gritted teeth. "Mum, look! It's some bloke! And he's got a gun!"

Edith looked. The man looked back, horror-struck. So far as Gonzalez knew, this scruffy little fat bloke and scrawny old woman weren't a part of Operation Harvest, so what on earth were they doing skulking around here in the bushes clutching big sticks? You didn't 'bump into people' in the Amazon rainforest! That sort of thing just didn't happen! The three of them were still gaping stupidly at each other in silent bewilderment when things got even more confusing. A stern-looking bald-headed man emerged, tiptoeing through the trees right between them. With his eyes darting from person to person, Max Wrench levelled his gun at Eric and glared.

"Who the hell are you?" he demanded, in an aggressive but hushed voice.

"What?" said Eric, glaring back. "Who the hell are YOU?"

Wrench had no patience for any of this nonsense. "That's none of your business!" he said. "Now you two just step aside. I'm only interested in the kid, OK?"

"Get lost!" blurted Eric. "If anyone's having him, it's me! That horrible little kid tried to kill me, he did!"

"And me!" said Edith, pointing to herself to make it clear who she was talking about.

Wrench raised an eyebrow. "Yeah? Well, join the club! He tried to kill me too!"

"Hey, don't forget me!" added Gonzalez.

It appeared the four of them had something in common. They were all convinced that the annoying boy on the other side of the bush was trying to kill them! And they all wanted their revenge.

Wrench decided to assert his authority. "Listen!" he hissed. "I'm here on official company business, understand? The kid is mine!"

"You can't have him, he's ours!" insisted Edith. "We've followed him for miles to get here!"

"Yeah!" added Eric, pointing to various cuts and little holes in his face. "Look what he did to me! I'm going to kill him!"

Gonzalez, normally a man of few words, wasn't going to stand for that. "No, you're not going to kill him! I am! I hate him more than you do!" he said, waving his gun in Eric's prickly face. "He set fire to me! And he pushed me in a piranha-infested river!"

"Huh? Is that all?" chipped in Wrench. "I spent three days and nights in the sea being towed behind a ship because of him! If anyone's going to kill him, it's me!"

Eric wasn't going to be outdone on the suffering front. "Hah! That's nothing! He's tried to kill me at least three times! Anyway, I saw him first! When I get my hands on him he's going to regret it!"

"Shhhh! Shut up, the lot of you!" interjected

Edith, "No one's going to kill him! He's worth millions, remember, and we've come all this way to kidnap him! I'm not going to let anyone ruin that now by bumping him off!"

Edith had the sort of commanding voice that wasn't easily ignored. It was a bit like someone jabbing the sharp end of a pencil into your ear and wiggling it around. The debate calmed down a little.

"Well as far as I'm concerned, you can have him," said Wrench, finally. "All I want from him is that map; then he's all yours."

Back in his camp, just the other side of a large shiny-leafed bush, Fintan was toasting another impaled sandwich.

"D'you want one, Gribs?" he said, pointing to the blackening object suspended over the fire. Gribley wasn't keen.

"No thank you, Master Fintan," he said. "I'm afraid I'm not terribly keen on peanut butter. Especially when charcoal coated."

"Ah! That reminds me!" said Fintan, snapping his fingers, having suddenly remembered what he'd stuffed somewhere near the bottom of his rucksack. "Well, how about some honey, then? I know you like a bit of honey, don't you!"

Gribley did indeed like a bit of honey on his toast. It was one of his great pleasures in life. Fintan unzipped his bag and rammed one arm in as far as it would go. With his tongue protruding from the side of his mouth, he felt around for a few moments before locating what he was looking for.

"Ta da!" he said, producing a large bent toothpaste tube. "Brilliant, eh!"

"Forgive me, sir," said Gribley, "but I was sure you mentioned honey, whereas the object you are holding would appear to be a large tube of minty toothpaste."

"Appear to be, yes, Gribs old friend, but appearances can be deceptive!" grinned Fintan, delighted at his own ingenuity. "When you told me I shouldn't bring anything in glass jars in case they broke, I had this brilliant idea! Honey in a tube! Don't worry, I rinsed it out really well before I put the honey in!"

Gribley had to admit that it was pretty clever,

though obviously not as clever as bringing a ready-made squeezy bottle of honey, which would have been easier and tasted a lot less minty.

"Ingenious, sir, and most resourceful! I would advise a degree of caution when unscrewing the cap, however, as the heat may have put the contents under pressure."

"Degree of caution, right," acknowledged Fintan, and yanked the top off the swollen tube. There was a loud popping noise as a large golden arc of warm honey sprayed into the air. Fintan struggled to control the tube as it shuddered in his hands like a fire hose.

"Whoops!" he said, and checked to see if there was anything left. There wasn't.

This was, of course, because it had all just landed on the heads, arms, shoulders and backs of the four conspiring figures crouching behind the shiny bush. With no idea what it was or where it had come from, they stared at each other in stunned silence. Intrigued, they inspected the dripping, sticky fluid, which had just fallen from the sky as if it were the sweet-smelling droppings of some exotic bird.

Whatever it was, it didn't appear to be dangerous.

A bit annoying, perhaps, but hardly life-threatening. In fact, had they not at that moment been hunched around a large ants' nest, it might not have proved much of a problem at all.

Eric was the first to realize something was wrong, when he felt some unpleasant activity occurring up his left trouser leg. He grimaced in pain and began jerking around as if he were being electrocuted. Before the other three had time to wonder what was happening to him, they found out for themselves. It appeared they had suddenly become very popular with several million huge, hungry ants. The ants poured out of the ground in a black, angry mass like boiling tar and swarmed all over them in a frenzy of little biting jaws. Edith let out a piercing screech which startled Fintan so much he dropped his toasted sandwich in the fire.

With a flurry of flailing arms and legs, the four sticky conspirators ran yelping and whimpering into the forest, desperately searching for a patch of mud or dirty little pool of water they could fling themselves into.

Undeterred, Fintan stuck another peanut butter

sandwich on his stick. "You're right, you know, Gribs," he observed, "some of the screeching noises do sound almost human, don't they!"

TWENTY-THREE

Later that evening, Wrench and Gonzalez set up their camp some distance away from the Bumsteads. They may have been on the same side, but neither pair trusted the other and besides, Wrench couldn't stand the smell. Eric and Edith had decided to spend the night wallowing in a muddy pool to help ease the pain of their ant bites. They were so distracted by the mass of little burning itches all over them that they didn't even notice they were sharing the pond with a few hundred leeches. Furious, miserable and wracked with pain, they sat in the mud and consoled themselves by imagining the violent things they would do to Fintan first thing in the morning.

Gonzalez and Max Wrench, meanwhile, were

attempting to apply ointment to some of their bites by torchlight when the satellite phone rang. It was Randall, and he wasn't happy.

"Wrench, listen to me," he hollered from the safety and comfort of his plush New York office. "You're making me look a fool here! You promised me you'd get the fruit and yet I'm not hearing any good news! There's a major publicity event under way here and you're coming up with nothing but excuses!"

"No, you listen to me," Wrench snarled back. "I told you I'd get to the fruit trees before the kid, and I will! Trust me, OK? This isn't easy, y'know!"

Randall wasn't listening. He was impatient to see results for his massive investment. The fact that he'd already notified the press about his "remarkable discovery" before having anything to show for it didn't help matters.

"Not easy? I'll tell you what's not easy, Mr Wrench – having to deal with the newspapers and the TV networks! That's not easy! I'm under immense pressure here to come up with something to show them and you're not providing it! It's all very well for you sitting around down there in the sunshine, Wrench, but this is really tough for me! If you want to keep your job, you'd better come up with the goods by tomorrow!"

This short but frank exchange of views did little to help Wrench's mood. He slammed the phone down and resumed dabbing at his injuries. By the time he crawled angrily into his sleeping bag, he had vowed that first thing in the morning he would take drastic action. Which he did.

Driven half-insane by another cold, uncomfortable night made worse by several hundred stinging ant bites, a mad-eyed Max Wrench rose at dawn, picked up his gun and set off intent on revenge. It was a dull, murky morning and pouring with incredibly heavy rain, which is fairly normal in a rainforest, but Wrench barely noticed. With a single-minded anger surging through his sleep-deprived mind, he squelched through the forest, focused intently on his mission. Fintan and Gribley were still fast asleep when he crashed into their camp.

"Get up, kid!" he bellowed. "This is your early-morning alarm call!"

Fintan groggily opened one eye and peered out through his mosquito net. There was a large, angry, bald-headed man with a goatee beard pointing a gun at him. Needless to say, this was a new experience.

"Get up, both of you!" repeated Wrench at full volume.

At that point it dawned on Fintan that he'd met the angry, shouty man before. He'd been on the ship with him. Though why he was now threatening them at gunpoint in the jungle wasn't immediately obvious.

"Why?" said Fintan, still half asleep. "What time is it?"

"Never mind what time it is, you dumb idiot! Just get out of there and put your hands up."

Fintan and Gribley clambered groggily down from their hammocks and did as they were told. Wearing only their pyjamas and wet socks, the pair of them stood in the tropical downpour with their hands up. Wrench was grinning dementedly and his gun arm was shaking with excitement. Gribley had absolutely no idea who the man was, or why he had so rudely awoken them.

Unbelievable as it seemed, they were about to be robbed by a strange bald-headed American man covered in cuts and scratches with mad staring eyes, in the middle of the Brazilian rainforest. Things like this only happened if you spent time with Fintan.

"Not so smart now, eh?" said Wrench, enjoying his sudden upper hand. "Not so brave now you've got a gun in your face, huh?"

Fintan was alarmed to say the least, and also a bit miffed, as he had been really enjoying his lie-in. "What do you want?" he asked, genuinely confused.

"Ha! Still think you're the funny kid, huh! You know exactly what I want and you're gonna give it to me, right now!"

Fintan still looked blank. Gribley looked even blanker. "I'm sorry, er, sir," he ventured cautiously, "but I'm afraid you may have mistaken us for some other people! I can assure you we have nothing of value."

"Shut up, flunkey!" barked Wrench, waving his gun around madly, then returned his attention to Fintan. "After all you've done to me, boy, you should consider yourself lucky I don't just kill you right here and now ... and your stupid flunkey guy too! I ought to let you die in this stinking jungle. No one would know! Now, open your bag real slow, and don't try any tricks, OK?"

Fintan stood with his hands above his head and sleepily wondered what he had in his bag that this horribly ill-looking man could possibly want. "Is it the sandwiches?" he asked, vaguely. "I've got plenty of them, so you're welcome to ha..."

"The map, dummy!" spat Wrench. "Give me the map!"

Fintan frowned. After all, this was the man who, only a few days earlier, had said the chocoplums were a big joke! The man who had laughed at him and made fun of him! But now, for some reason, he'd completely changed his mind. Fintan didn't like him one bit and certainly didn't want to give him the map.

"No. Why should I?" he said, more out of stupidity than bravery.

Wrench steadied the gun in both hands and aimed at Fintan's face. "Because if you don't gimme the map, I'm gonna shoot you."

Fintan considered this for a moment, exchanged glances with Gribley and decided it seemed like a pretty good reason. Reluctantly, he ferreted around in his bag and produced Ana's crumpled sheet of paper. Without lowering his gun for a moment, Wrench snatched it from him.

"Now that's the first sensible thing you've done, kid!" he said triumphantly, and began backing away into the jungle. "Listen up: if you try and follow me, I'll shoot you dead, understand? I've got the map now so you don't stand a chance. I get the fruit trees and you losers get to wander round lost in this big old jungle till you die. You made me suffer; now it's your turn!"

Still grinning like a maniac and staring with his horribly bloodshot eyes, Wrench disappeared into the thick undergrowth and was gone.

Apart from the steady drumming of heavy rain on the jungle foliage, silence returned to Fintan's camp. They put their arms down and stood motionless in stunned surprise.

"Were you acquainted with the American gentleman, sir?" enquired Gribley. "He appeared to be quite familiar with you."

"Well, not really, Gribs. I did meet him on the ship, though. He works for some big cake company."

Gribley still wasn't clear why an apparent stranger who turned out to be a business rival would appear from nowhere, take their map and threaten to kill them. "It appeared you had done something to rather upset him, sir. Do you recall what that might have been?"

"Beats me," shrugged Fintan. "All I did was spoil his dinner a bit. Knocked his wine over. Nothing serious or anything! Bit of an overreaction, if you ask me! He must really like that lobster thermostat stuff!"

After a while, they attempted to find some dry clothes, get themselves organized and consider what they were going to do next. There was no doubt in Fintan's mind that this was a major blow. Losing the map had ruined everything. Not only had they lost all chance of getting to the chocoplums, they were now stuck in the middle of the biggest rainforest on earth with no idea of the way out!

"What are we going to do without a map, Gribs?" said Fintan, sounding extremely worried.

"Ah, that's not a problem, sir," announced Gribley with his usual calm. "I thought it might be wise to make a copy in case the original were to be lost. There's one rolled up in my pack."

Fintan clapped Gribley on the back. "Brilliant!" he said. "What would I do without you, eh, Gribs?"

TWENTY-FOUR

Wrench grinned madly at the scruffy little hand-drawn map in his trembling hands, switched on his satellite phone and took out his very expensive digital camera. The directions Ana had drawn weren't very clear, but he was able to recognize some distinct features which corresponded with his map of the area. He took a photograph of it, then relayed the image to "Operation Harvest Field HQ", which had been hurriedly assembled on the outskirts of Santos Coelho. Giganti-Foods International had flown in enough men, weaponry, heavy machinery and computer equipment to start a small war, and now, it seemed, they finally had the information they needed to spring into action.

A small group of technicians fired up their solar-powered laptops and a digital image of the map was superimposed over their existing satellite data. It was cross-checked and an approximate grid reference was quickly established. There was a flurry of activity, and within minutes an advance helicopter mission was dispatched to the grove's coordinates to establish visual confirmation.

"Keep me informed, OK!" said Wrench to one of the technicians at Field HQ. "I wanna direct the operation from the front line, so come get me as soon as we get word from the advance mission!"

The plan that Max Wrench and Randall T. Buckmeister had devised between them was simple, nasty and selfish. As soon as the grove was located, they would drop in a ground clearance force from helicopters, who would hack out a massive landing area with chainsaws. Because of the huge distances involved, they would need to set up several refuelling points in the jungle and organize almost constant supply trips back and forth to base camp, but as money was no object and environmental damage didn't particularly bother them, this was no problem.

Wrench would then be located, winched up and flown to the grove to take command. He would make sure the area was thoroughly searched and mapped to make sure nothing was missed. It was, after all, a TOTAL removal mission. Soil samples would be taken and the air temperature and humidity levels recorded. Generators would be winched into position and powerful arc lamps erected for security. Perimeter guards with enormous guns would patrol the area in case of "incursions from their competitors", which basically meant shooting Fintan Fedora if he came too close.

The next stage would involve another wave of larger helicopters, which would bring in the machinery for carefully uprooting every single one of the trees, packaging them and preparing them for transit.

The final, and nastiest, phase of Operation Harvest would involve destroying any possibility of the trees springing up again, in case someone else got their hands on them. The ground would be "neutralized" with flame-throwers. Burnt, pulverized, poisoned and left completely lifeless. The world of fruit cakes was, as previously mentioned, a very, very serious business!

The angry, impatient phone calls from Randall T. Buckmeister had been getting more and more frequent, so it was with some pleasure that Wrench prepared to report this great advance back to head office. He was just reaching for the satellite phone when the red channel rang. It was Barbara.

"How did you get through on this line?" demanded Wrench. "This is for top-secret communications only!"

"Never you mind how I got the number, Max," said Barbara's grating voice. "I just wanted to call to let you know that I'm having a wonderful time without you! Right now I'm relaxing in the beautiful Rio de Janeiro sunshine. I'm lying on a lounger beside my luxury hotel's luxury pool and I'm drinking my third piña colada! It's luxury, you hear?"

Riveting as this was, Wrench had no interest in listening to his annoying wife rub his nose in it any further. "Yeah, yeah! Not now, Barbara!" he barked. "You gotta get off the line! I need to speak to Randall urgently!"

He hung up and punched in the number for Mission HQ.

"Randall?" he announced triumphantly. "Operation Harvest is under way!"

TWENTY-FIVE

The mood in Fintan's little expedition was low. They had made virtually no progress during the miserable rain-soaked day and a feeling of hopeless dejection had crept over them. All hope of being the first to reach the chocoplums had gone. They had lost. Worse still, they had lost because Fintan hadn't managed to keep his mouth shut and had blurted out the secret to a complete stranger. He trudged wearily through the mud, imagining what Correntina would say if she knew what was about to happen to her beloved secret grove – and even more scarily, what Ana would do to him if she found out!

Evening fell and there was still no let-up in the torrential rain. They stopped and made camp again. There was no dry wood anywhere, so all hopes of putting the kettle on for a nice cup of tea and having something warm to eat had to be forgotten again. Fintan sheltered with Gribley under a waterproof tarpaulin, listening to the relentless tropical downpour. He sighed. All conversation had fizzled out hours before and had been replaced by a sort of mutual dull grey resignation.

An hour or so later they had set up their hammocks, covered them in the plastic sheet and eaten a few boring dried rations. Fintan was just hauling the iron cooking pot up a tree when he realized the rain was finally stopping.

"About time, too!" he said.

It was only when the rain's constant hammering noise had completely faded that they became aware of other, much less natural, sounds. Not very far away, something was making a sort of deep, vibrating roar, like a nasty mechanical cough. There were creaking and sweeping noises and thundering crashes. They stared at each other for a moment before understanding what it was.

"Chainsaws!" said Fintan, raising his eyebrows in horror. "They're cutting down the chocoplum trees!"

Hurriedly, they grabbed their head torches and

fumbled through the dark undergrowth towards the terrible sound. It appeared to be very close by, just the other side of a high ridge of ground. Gribley, anxious that they shouldn't get lost, had tied a bit of string to the end of his hammock and was gradually feeding it out as they went.

An unnaturally brilliant light illuminated the horizon, and shone eerily through the trees. They scrambled up to the top of the muddy bank and gazed down the other side at a horrible, stomach-turning sight. What had once been Correntina's beautiful secret valley now looked like a war zone. In the glare of several powerful arc lamps erected around the site's perimeter, Giganti-Foods International's huge mechanical diggers were busy destroying the grove, while three massive black cargo helicopters sat like hungry crows waiting to carry the uprooted trees back to their nests. What had until very recently been untouched rainforest was now a mess of men, mud and logging equipment. The air around them throbbed with the noise of generators and was filled with the smell of petrol fumes, wet wood and disturbed earth.

At least a dozen men wearing bright red "Giganti-

Foods" boiler suits were packing the felled trees into sheets of plastic and loading them into metal containers. Others were putting the finishing touches to a temporary corrugated iron hut, and several more were hacking at the remaining tree roots with a variety of heavy machinery. Standing proudly right in the middle of the carnage was Max Wrench himself, pointing and shouting orders and apparently enjoying himself enormously.

Fintan and Gribley's jaws dropped in shared horror. This was terrible! It was all over! For some time they crouched on the brow of the hill and watched in stunned silence, with no idea what to say or do. Fintan fought back a tear. If Correntina and Ana could see this, they would be heartbroken ... and would probably want to kill him too!

Eventually the bulldozers' engines were turned off and the men gradually stopped work for the night. Wrench congratulated his team on a fine day's work and disappeared with them into the small hut for an excellent evening meal and a lot of showing off. Only a pair of security guards remained active, patrolling the edge of the site and occasionally pointing their guns into the surrounding forest.

"I'm going down there, Gribs," said Fintan resolutely. "I've got to try and find a chocoplum before they take the lot!"

Gribley was, understandably, not keen on the idea.

"You do realize, sir, that there are men with guns down there? And that they have been instructed to shoot you on sight?"

"Yeah, I know," said Fintan. "But . . . but it's what we came all this way for, isn't it? I'm not letting that greedy lot take them all! That's just plain selfish!"

After a short pause and some careful thought, Gribley found himself agreeing. They had indeed come a long way and put up with all manner of hardships to get this close to their prize. It was an incredibly dangerous thing to attempt, especially for someone as accident-prone as Fintan, but to turn around and leave now would be unforgivable. "Very well, sir," he said, "but I insist on coming with you."

The slope down into the grove wasn't too steep but was extremely muddy and dotted with little prickly bushes, which gave them a little bit of cover and a lot of prickles. Cautiously, they slithered down through the soggy earth and leaf litter until they reached the last of the bushes and peered out into the grove ... or what was left of it. The bright lights erected around the perimeter meant they had a perfectly clear view of its mangled, ripped-up remains. From close up it looked even worse.

Every single one of the trees had completely gone. In only a few hours Wrench's team of highly trained thugs had taken the whole lot and left nothing but a few scattered branches, muddy leaves and twisted roots. The two security guards were now chatting together and walking casually around the devastation, looking very pleased with themselves. Judging by the way they were swaggering about, Fintan guessed they weren't actually expecting anyone to sneak past them. They were, after all, hidden in a secret valley, deep in the middle of the world's biggest rainforest, protecting a few trees which hardly anyone believed in! And they had big guns! All of which meant they weren't paying much attention to their jobs. This, of course, was good news for Fintan, who wasn't known for his stealth.

When the guards strolled to the other side of the site, Fintan and Gribley (who had tied his length of string to the prickly bush) made their move. Together they crept into the glare of the lights, across the bare ground, and hid behind a large tank of fuel. From this vantage point they had an even better view of the whole ugly scene. None of the trees were accessible. Every single one had been wrapped and loaded for transit. Their only chance of finding any fruit was to scour the mess littering the ground. Even that didn't look very promising.

"Look!" hissed Gribley eventually, pointing towards one of the parked diggers. "Over there, beneath that vehicle! I think those branches still have some fruit on!"

Fintan looked, and for the first time in his life, laid eyes on the great Brazilian chocoplum! It was real! A bit battered, perhaps, and lying in the mud churned up by the digger's caterpillar tracks, but definitely real! Reddish brown and shiny, like a big soft conker, just like the magazine had described it!

"Brilliant!" he whispered, and a big relieved grin appeared on his face. They may have been beaten by the might and wealth of Giganti-Foods International, but if he could just get one chocoplum safely home and plant the seed, then all was not lost!

Crawling on their hands and knees, Fintan and Gribley made their way through the mud from one hiding place to another, until they reached the bent and broken branch under the huge mechanical digger. There was at least one undamaged fruit still dangling from it, and a handful of sad-looking specimens lying around, trampled underfoot.

Carefully, and with a rush of great excitement, Fintan picked the chocoplum and held it reverently in the palm of his hand. It was surprisingly heavy for its size and shone beautifully in the glaring security lights. It had the soft, fuzzy texture of a peach. Immensely pleased to finally have one of these fabulous objects in his possession, he slipped it into his jacket pocket and searched around in case there were any others.

Suddenly, Gribley tapped him on the shoulder. The guards were now walking in their direction, but appeared not to have noticed them. Holding their breath, the two intruders crouched in the shadows beneath the digger and hoped they wouldn't be spotted. They heard the armed men chatting about what a brilliant job they had and how much they were getting paid, then watched their red-uniformed legs and big heavy boots pass within a few yards. Fintan winced as he watched one of them take a casual kick at a half-squashed chocoplum that was lying in his path. These hooligans didn't deserve to have their hands on these precious fruits! It wasn't right and it wasn't fair!

When the danger seemed to have passed, Fintan returned his attention to searching for any remaining fruits. It looked hopeless. Even if there were any others lying around, they were out in open ground, which meant being spotted and probably being shot. Apart from the one in his pocket, every single chocoplum in the world was now either destroyed or locked up inside a massive metal container, bolted beneath a Giganti-Foods helicopter.

It was time to go. Keeping a careful eye on the security guards, they slowly made their way back to the safety of the dark bushes.

"Ah, well," sighed Fintan, disappointed but not entirely defeated. "At least we've got something to take home!"

Gribley nodded in agreement, untied the end of his bit of string and began climbing back up the muddy slope to camp.

"Wait, hang on a second! I've just thought of something!" said Fintan. Much to Gribley's surprise, he crept back to the big metal fuel tank. It appeared he'd found a rather bent-looking petrol can on the ground, which, by the look of it, had been run over at least once. He held it up for Gribley to see and gave a thumbs-up sign, then began filling it from the tap on the side of the petrol tank. Confused, Gribley waited in the bushes for him to return.

"Nice cup of tea!" said Fintan, when he got back. "We can make a fire now, and have hot food and tea and everything! That'll cheer us up, won't it!"

TWENTY-SIX

Having followed Gribley's string trail all the way back to their camp, Fintan's first thought was to put the chocoplum somewhere safe. He extracted one of his many little plastic boxes from his rucksack, wrapped the precious fruit in a page torn from *Young Adventurer* magazine and carefully sealed it inside.

"There!" he said. "All safe! Nothing left to do now but head home, I suppose."

"Indeed, sir," agreed Gribley, sounding relieved to hear the word "home" mentioned. "I still have the copy of the map, so may I suggest we make our way back to Ana's boat first thing tomorrow morning?"

"Fine idea, Gribs!" said Fintan. "Or at least, first thing after breakfast! Which reminds me ... let's get that fire going and have a bit of supper, eh?"

The can of petrol he had borrowed from Giganti-Foods International's supply tank was a lot lighter than he remembered it being. On closer inspection he noticed a jagged hole in the bottom, which was leaking its flammable contents on to the damp ground. Luckily, there was still enough left to get a campfire started, which was all they needed, after all. Fintan made a pile of logs and kindling exactly as his favourite magazine recommended, then poured the last of the petrol over it.

"Can I have the matches, please, Gribs?" he said.

Gribley, who was selecting a few useful dried food items from the cooking pot, thought it would probably be safer if he lit the fire himself. Fintan didn't have a very good track record in the fire safety department. It wasn't just the odd barbecue, garden shed and scout hut which had gone up in flames, but now strange men's beards had to be added to the list.

"Perhaps I should do it, sir," he said, and made sure Fintan was standing well away and hadn't spilt petrol all over himself. As it turned out, the campfire lit beautifully and without a problem.

"See!" announced Fintan proudly. "I can get things right sometimes, can't I!"

Gribley conceded this point and happily began preparing another tasty stew for their supper. What both of them had failed to notice, however, was the trail of burning petrol they'd just ignited, which led from their camp and snaked off into the darkness of the forest.

Just under a mile away, Max Wrench, Gonzalez and his twenty other Giganti-Foods employees were sitting comfortably inside their corrugated iron hut digesting their victory meal.

"I'd like to propose a toast!" announced Wrench. "To a job well done! Congratulations, guys! We did it!"

Glasses were clinked and a lot of self-congratulatory whooping and cheering ensued. Wrench couldn't remember ever feeling quite so happy. He had just harvested the entire crop of Brazilian chocoplums, thereby exclusively securing the world's rarest and most delicious fruit for Giganti-Foods International! His boss was going to be so pleased that he was bound to give him a promotion and a raise in salary! Not only that, but his horrible, irritating wife, Barbara, had finally gone off and left him alone to concentrate on his true love: his career and the pursuit of money!

Better than all this, though, was the knowledge that he'd beaten that Fedora kid to the prize! He had his revenge. Feeling extremely pleased with himself, he said goodnight to his men and left the hut to make a satellite call to Buckmeister's New York office. He was just dialling the number and imagining how good it would feel to say the words "mission accomplished" to Randall when he noticed a strange fiery snake zigzagging its way down the hill into the valley.

"Hey!" he shouted to the two useless security guards who were now sitting on a log drinking coffee. "What the hell's that?"

Whatever it was, it appeared to be heading at top speed towards their fuel supply. It was moving so quickly, in fact, that before the guards had a chance to investigate, it had reached the tank and burned its way to the still-dribbling tap. There was a sudden blinding flash of light as the heavy iron tank ripped itself apart and erupted in a huge orange fireball.

The noise that followed a fraction of a second later was like a clap of thunder. Wrench and the inept guards were thrown flat on their backs. They lay there stunned, watching the gigantic mass of flame billowing into the night sky. A wall of hot air swept over them and singed their eyebrows.

Gonzalez and the rest of the men came running out of the hut and stared in amazement at the chaos. At that moment another massive blast launched a substantial chunk of burning iron into the air, forcing the horrified men to scatter and run for cover.

Then suddenly, the part of wrecked fuel tank fell to earth like a meteor. With a terrifying deep whooshing sound it crashed on to the cockpit of one of the helicopters, which crumpled and burst into flames. Everyone was frightened out of their wits. There was absolutely nothing they could do. The savagely roaring ball of fire quickly spread to two nearby diggers, which instantly exploded in a mass of burning debris.

"Sabotage!" shouted Wrench, running as fast as he could for the safety of the forest. "We've been sabotaged!"

Confused and terrified, the men quickly

abandoned the camp too. They followed Wrench into the trees, dodging lumps of flaming machinery which were falling from the sky like giant hailstones. Behind them, another helicopter blew up, taking its priceless cargo of chocoplum trees with it in a vivid plume of fire. It flipped violently into the air, landing on its back and crushing the power generator. With a shower of sparks and jagged electrical noises the entire ring of security lights went out.

A terrible red glow illuminated the jungle clearing, as one by one, all their highly expensive machines succumbed to the inferno. A caterpillar-tracked digger was hurled sideways, wiping out the hut where the men had just been sitting. Tables, chairs and the remains of their evening meal were instantly reduced to flying fragments. Wrench stared with utter disbelief at the mess. His entire chocoplum harvest was gone! As was his accommodation, his food supply, his transport, his tracking gear . . . and his whole professional future!

It was only then that he realized he was still holding the satellite phone in his sweaty, trembling hand and that Randall's furious voice was shrieking from it! Hurriedly, he switched the phone off. This was no time to be dealing with his boss! The last of the helicopters burst into shreds of metal, scattering itself across the blackened wasteland of what had been the chocoplum grove. There was now nothing left at all! Just a huge burning pile of wreckage. Wrench was mortified.

Not five minutes earlier he'd been sharing a celebratory bottle of champagne with his men and feeling happier than he could ever remember. Now this! This was the worst possible thing that could have happened to him! A complete disaster!

After waking to find Fintan's camp deserted, the Bumstead's had spent the day picking leeches off themselves and scratching. Now less than a mile away, they were startled by a sudden thundering noise and lights in the sky. Neither of them had eaten all day and had barely moved either. Eric raised his horribly swollen and mud-caked face from the ground.

"Is that fireworks?" he muttered.

"How should I know?" snapped his mother, who was too busy scratching her armpit to pay any attention.

Eric slumped back down again. The hunger and the fatigue and the constant terrible itching had been driving him insane. Now it seemed they were making him see things too! They didn't have firework displays in the rainforest! How crazy! He must have imagined it!

The devastating destruction of Operation Harvest, which had just ruined Max Wrench's entire life, had also slightly annoyed Fintan and Gribley. It had interrupted their supper.

"Good grief, what are they doing now?" complained Fintan, as a huge lurid orange plume of fire lit up the sky and booming explosions scared every bird for miles around out of the trees. "Haven't they done enough damage for one day without blowing things up as well?" He wiped up the last of his stew with a peanut butter sandwich, tutted in disapproval and rolled his eyeballs.

"Absolutely, sir," agreed Gribley. "It would appear our business rivals have very little consideration for the natural world. I really don't approve of their methods."

Fintan nodded sadly. "Nor do I, Gribs! Bullies,

194

that's what they are! Big, ignorant bullies!"

They sat drinking their mugs of steaming tea and disapprovingly watched the continuing fire show illuminate the darkness and disrupt the peace of the forest.

"Better get some kip, then," said Fintan, and started packing their dinner things away.

By the time he'd finished hoisting the cooking pot stuffed with their remaining food supply up a tree, the nearby fire storm seemed to have burned itself out.

"Well, I just hope they're proud of themselves! That's all I can say!" he said as he climbed into his hammock.

"Indeed. Goodnight, Master Fintan, sir," added Gribley, who was already zipped into his sleeping bag and busy flicking the insects out of his mosquito net. "Sleep well. We've got an early start in the morning."

TWENTY-SEVEN

"Think, you idiots!" yelled a red-faced Max Wrench at his cowering security guards. "Did you see anyone come into the camp? Did you see a kid?"

The two guards shook their heads guiltily and looked terrified. "No, sir, Mr Wrench, sir," they each stammered in turn. "We definitely didn't see anyone."

"You're sure? You're completely sure?" continued Wrench, looking as if he were about to explode in a similar way to the fuel tank. They nodded adamantly.

Wrench knew it was Fintan, though. It had to have been Fintan! Why else would his entire operation suddenly disappear in a ball of fire in a soaking-wet jungle? It was sabotage, all right. Mind you, even Wrench found himself a little shocked by the depths the kid seemed prepared to stoop to. He'd just destroyed every single chocoplum in the world rather than let his rivals have them! That was pretty ruthless! With an attitude like that, he could have a glittering career ahead of him at Giganti-Foods International!

Talking of Giganti-Foods, the satellite phone's red channel rang. There was no more avoiding it. It was time to explain the night's rather tricky developments to Randall. Dreading what he was about to hear, Wrench answered the call.

"What the hell was all that noise?" demanded a furious-sounding Randall T. Buckmeister. "What's going on down there?"

"Er, listen, Randall. Things aren't too good at the moment," began Wrench. "We've had a bit of a setback...."

"A setback?" screamed Buckmeister. "That sounded like more than just a setback to me, Wrench! It sounded like some kind of war going on! Just tell me one thing, OK? Tell me you have the chocoplums safe?"

"Well ... not exactly," ventured Wrench, steeling himself for the expected volley of insults.

"Not exactly? You either have them or you don't!" bellowed Randall. "Now you listen to me, Mr So-Called Jungle Explorer – I've had it with your excuses! This is the real jungle, right here! The business jungle! Do you understand? I've got a multimillion-dollar advertising campaign bought and paid for! Newspapers, magazines, internet, radio, TV . . . you name it! I've got the press calling me all the time wanting to know the big secret, and I've got nothing to tell them! I've even got people making jokes about me, Wrench! They're accusing me of making the whole thing up! Tell me you've secured these fruits right now, Wrench, or you're FINISHED!"

A few yards away, Gonzalez and the rest of the men sat miserably amid the smoking ruins, pretending they weren't listening to the conversation. It wasn't sounding good. Their boss had gone from triumph to ruin in less than half an hour, and judging by the look on his face, the news wasn't being received well back in New York. They watched as a stunned-looking Max Wrench dropped the phone to the ground and let out a loud, anguished yell. It was the yell of a highly ambitious, highly paid, highly successful businessman who had just got the sack. He probably wasn't going to be in a very good mood.

Seconds later, Wrench came striding towards them, his smoke-blackened face twisted into a terrifying snarl.

"Gimme that gun!" he hollered. "And that one! In fact, gimme all the guns we've got left! I'm gonna sort this out right now!"

Reluctantly, the security guards handed over their weapons, half expecting their boss to begin shooting everyone in sight, which luckily he didn't. Instead, Wrench slung the heavy rifles over his shoulder and filled his pockets with revolvers and enough ammunition to wipe out a small country. He even snatched up a slightly bent-looking flame-thrower which had somehow survived the disaster, then, without saying another word, headed off to the bottom of the muddy slope. There, he switched on his powerful torch, located the burnt petrol trail on the ground and began following it into the darkness.

Happily snoring the night away in his cosy explorer's pyjamas, Fintan was dreaming of home. He was dreaming of the hero's welcome he was going to receive when he showed his doubting family the fabulous little brown fruit he'd brought back from the other side of the world! He could see the looks of surprise and admiration on their faces and feel the congratulatory handshakes! They were all gathering around him and his trophy and expressing their amazement and what he could achieve when trusted with an important mission!

Gribley was dreaming of home too. He was lying in a wonderful hot, bubbly bath with a china cup of speciality tea and a large plate of honey on toast, cut into nice little triangles.

Meanwhile, out in the jungle night, a furious bald-headed man with more guns than sense was following the path of burnt undergrowth to their camp. He had lost everything, including all sense of proportion and most of his mind. His torchlight finally fell on a pair of gently swaying hammocks. He grinned a nasty, twisted grin and raised one of his guns. It was time for his ultimate and final revenge!

However, immediately above him in a dark

tree, Fintan's best attempt at knot-tying was gradually undoing itself. With impeccable timing, the knot finally let go of its heavy load. The oversized iron cooking pot cracked down on to Wrench's unsuspecting head with the force of a charging rhino. Everything went black. Knocked out instantly, he hit the ground and lay sprawled amid the pot's contents, which spilled out on to the forest floor. A variety of hungry little creatures discovered the sudden feast and climbed all over him, attracted by the smell of food.

In his deep, blissful sleep, Fintan heard a loud clanging noise, which oddly enough came from a popping champagne cork.

"Congratulations, son!" his father was saying. "I'm so proud of you!"

When dawn broke in the rainforest, Gribley was, as usual, the first one awake. He rubbed his eyes, stretched and remembered that this was the day they were going to begin heading home. Cheered by this happy thought, he climbed down from his hammock and considered making a hearty breakfast. Unfortunately there was no food left. The lidless cooking pot lay upturned on the ground, surrounded by empty food packets, apparently ripped open and with all the contents eaten! Even more surprisingly, there was a large, smoke-stained, bald man lying flat on his back covered in guns and animal poo. This, unfortunately, meant breakfast was off.

"Master Fintan, sir," said Gribley, shaking the sleeping boy awake, "I think perhaps you should see this."

"Five more minutes, Gribs..." Fintan mumbled from inside his sleeping bag.

"No, now, please, sir. This is quite important," insisted Gribley.

When he was eventually persuaded to forgo his lie-in and get up, Fintan was stunned.

"Him again! What's on earth's he doing here?" he said sleepily, not fully understanding what was going on.

"I'm not sure, sir," said Gribley. "I found him lying there a moment ago. I think he's asleep ... or possibly unconscious. He's not dead, though. I checked his pulse."

Fintan surveyed the mess of empty food wrappers.

"Has he been nicking our food? Oh no, he's been nicking our food, hasn't he!"

"I couldn't say for sure, sir," said Gribley, "but I'm afraid it's true that we are now completely out of rations."

The shock of this news soon had Fintan wide awake.

"What?" he said, appalled. "No food? Not even breakfast? We'll starve!"

In a slightly downbeat mood, Fintan and Gribley silently packed away all their gear (with the exception of the iron pot, which they no longer had any use for) and prepared for their homeward journey. Without so much as a single cup of tea inside them, they shouldered their packs once again and wondered what to do with their sleeping visitor.

"Leave him there!" said Fintan grumpily. "I expect he'll wake up with a terrible stomachache after eating all our food! Serves him right too, the greedy devil!"

Gribley produced the map and the compass and led the way into the trees.

"Seriously, though, Gribs," said a worried-sounding Fintan. "What are we going to eat? We're in big trouble, aren't we?"

Gribley sounded a lot less concerned. "As luck would have it, sir, I once read a particularly useful book on jungle survival techniques. It said we can drink rainwater, which will keep us alive. Food is of less importance than water, but the book also included advice on which insects one can safely eat. Apparently providing one avoids the hairiest and most brightly coloured insects, the rest are quite safe. Termites, worms and all manner of bugs are perfectly edible. Grasshoppers are particularly favoured, I believe, once the heads, wings and legs have been removed."

Fintan was thoroughly disgusted. "You know you can read too many books, don't you, Gribley?" he said, pulling a face.

A moment later he appeared to remember something important, stopped, dropped his pack and began rummaging through his washbag.

"However, Gribs old friend, you'll be pleased to hear that this time, it's me that's done something clever! Look! I hid a peanut butter sandwich wrapped up in my flannel in case of emergencies!

See! We can cut it into little pieces and ration it!"

Feeling very proud of himself, Fintan took out his penknife and carefully cut the sandwich into sixteen tiny, equal squares. These were then reverently wrapped in a page torn from *Young Adventurer* magazine and placed in one of his little plastic boxes for safe keeping.

Gribley cast an eye over the soggy emergency sandwich. There were a few bits of soap stuck to it and it was almost completely squashed.

"Indeed, sir," he said flatly. "We're saved!"

TWENTY-EIGHT

It was late afternoon by the time Gonzalez and a few of the other men found Wrench and were puzzled as to why he should be lying flat on his back by an empty iron cooking pot. They revived him with a little water, patched up the nasty cut on his head and escorted him back to the burnt remains of their camp.

By the time he was lucid enough to speak, it became clear that Wrench had no idea what had happened either. All he could remember was that he was going on a lovely vacation to Brazil and kept asking where Barbara was. He had no memory at all of the chocoplum mission or of the explosions which had destroyed it. Everything was a blank.

Gonzalez decided he should probably take

command. He picked up Wrench's satellite phone and called the emergency services to ask for help. It turned out that the local authorities were already extremely busy. Apparently they were overstretched due to a major manhunt. Most of their resources were tied up looking for the "vicious hot dog-van thieves". Gonzalez decided to mention that among his party was his boss, Senor Wrench, who was seriously injured. Just in case it might help, he added that Senor Wrench was very rich and would be very grateful.

It helped. The woman on the phone couldn't write their map coordinates down quickly enough. Within an hour, help was on its way. A huge police rescue helicopter with a paramedic on board was hurriedly dispatched out over the jungle looking for a clearing full of burnt rubble and twenty-two hopelessly lost men.

Gribley, on the other hand, knew exactly where he was and where he was going. He was going home! Spurred on by this tantalizing prospect, he and Fintan – without the heavy cooking pot – had made good progress. According to the map, they could expect to reach the river before nightfall. Everything was going according to plan for a change. After what they hoped would be a good night's sleep on the riverbank, they planned to take Ana's boat back upstream the following day. Quite how they were going to paddle it against the current was something Gribley was trying not to think about. It hadn't yet occurred to Fintan.

For the rest of the day they pressed on through the dense forest, putting up with its now-familiar hardships. There was the usual stifling heat to deal with, and the added difficulty of having to collect rainwater to drink. There was the humidity, more torrential rain, the mud, and the constant danger of falling branches, which would drop unexpectedly from the canopy above. There was also the awkward moment when Fintan pulled down a springy branch, let it go and launched a long stripy snake which wrapped itself around Gribley's neck like a scarf.

But worst of all was the hunger. By evening Fintan's stomach was making regular gurgling noises loud enough to startle parrots. He had politely declined to try any of the little snacks Gribley had plucked from the trees and was feeling horribly weak. Not weak enough to eat insects yet, but horribly weak all the same.

The relief he felt when they eventually reached the river was enormous. They had even managed to arrive before sunset, which meant they could still see to pitch their camp.

"Well done, sir," commended Gribley, as Fintan dropped his pack and lay in a heap on the ground. "We've done a good day's walking, even though I say so myself!"

Fintan forced a weary smile but couldn't muster any conversation. Gribley had a quick scout around in case he'd confused their location somehow, but he was confident it was the same spot where they had arrived a few days earlier: a large, clear muddy area with virtually no trees, which meant they could see the sky for a change. There were the same tall pink rocks split by a cascading waterfall, the same merging of rivers and the same turbulent brown water. The only difference was that the river level had risen considerably, probably because of all the rain . . . and their boat had gone. This was bad. With an unpleasantly cold feeling of doom growing in his stomach, he frantically double-checked the area, and even looked up the trees, but it had definitely gone. Floated away in the high water. This wasn't going to be easy news to break.

"What?" said Fintan when he eventually realized Gribley wasn't joking. "Gone? But how did it... I mean, but ... what are we going to do now?"

A painful silence followed. This was a question that neither of them could answer. "Die" was the only obvious word they could come up with, and neither of them wanted to say it. With heavy legs and even heavier hearts, they tied their hammocks in silence and prepared for the fast-approaching night. Gribley couldn't even bring himself to gather a crunchy little supper. This was a new low point.

They sat side by side on a log for a while and miserably shared a tiny square of soapy peanut butter sandwich. Neither of them spoke, each quietly contemplating the dire new situation they found themselves in. They may have made it to the chocoplum grove and got something to show for it, but their chances of getting home alive had suddenly got a lot slimmer. As had Fintan's stomach, which gurgled in protest at its diminished rations.

"Gribs," said Fintan after a while, "if we do manage to get out of here ... you know, if we get home OK ... will you remind me to write a letter to Correntina and Ana? I think I ought to apologize. I mean, we've lost the boat now, as well as the chocoplum grove! They're not going to be very happy with me!"

Gribley managed to force a fairly positive-sounding tone. "Of course, sir. As soon as we're home I'll remind you to write."

"Thanks, Gribs, old mate," said Fintan listlessly. "Shame, really. It's all ended up as a bit of a mess, hasn't it! Hardly any food left, no boat, no way home! Still, at least things can't get any worse!"

Approximately four hours later, things got worse. Fintan, tossing from side to side in restless sleep, began dreaming of food. Irresistibly tempting visions floated before him. Vast mountains of mashed potato with sausages sticking out of them and floods of ketchup dribbling down the sides. Big bagfuls of fat greasy chips smelling of vinegar. Slabs of fruit cake as big as house bricks, steaming hot chocolate puddings drowning in gallons of chocolate sauce, whole jars of peanut butter dolloped on to thick, crusty white bread. He was suffering from the dreaded night starvation! Without knowing what he was doing, Fintan began sleep-eating. Just before dawn he awoke feeling a lot less hungry than when he went to sleep and with his hand in an empty plastic container.

"Oh no!" he yelled, startling Gribley awake. "Oh no! What have I done!"

As far as Gribley was concerned, it wasn't such a terrible thing. Fintan had been welcome to the emergency soapy sandwich. It wasn't all that important, really, in the scheme of things. They were probably going to starve anyway. The only thing he found annoying was having to listen to his endless stream of abject apologies.

"Oh, Gribs! I'm so sorry!" wailed Fintan. "Please believe me! I didn't mean to do it! We were going to share that last sandwich and I ate the lot! I'm so sorry! I'm sorry! I couldn't help it! I was asleep! Please forgive me!"

Gribley gritted his teeth. It was possible that he

only had a short while left to live and he didn't really want to spend his last few hours on earth listening to this irritating racket.

"Master Fintan, sir," he said with uncharacteristic abruptness, "will you kindly shut up, please!"

TWENTY-NINE

Eric and Edith Bumstead had, as usual, spent the night hungry, thirsty, lost and lying uncomfortably on the ground being bitten by insects. This particular night, though, they had, for some reason, been bitten a lot less than normal. It was either because they had slept on some warm pink rocks by the bank of a river, or more likely because they smelled so hideous by this stage that even the mosquitoes were avoiding them.

Eric was just contemplating whether he could be bothered to sit up and face another day when he thought he heard a voice. It was someone telling someone to shut up – only for once it wasn't his mother speaking! It was a man!

Unless, of course, he was imagining it. After

wandering around in the jungle for several days in the company of his offensively sharp-tongued mother and living off bugs, berries and nuts, he had begun imagining all sorts of things. The firework display had been weird enough, but it had got worse. More than once he'd thought he heard seagulls or possibly penguins, neither of which was very likely in the rainforest! The previous afternoon he'd even seen a pink ice-cream van parked under a tree! This voice, however, had sounded very real and very close by. He forced his grubby, sun-blistered eyes open, got to his feet and looked around. Less than a hundred yards away, on the edge of the clearing, there were two hammocks suspended from the trees. And standing next to the hammocks were two very familiar-looking people who appeared to be involved in some sort of argument.

"Mum!" he said, shaking her roughly by the shoulder. "Mum, wake up! You're not going to believe this!"

"Well, there's no need to be rude!" moaned Fintan miserably. "I was only trying to be nice!"

Gribley let out a sigh, and apologized. "I'm sorry

too, Master Fintan. I'm afraid our difficult situation is causing us both to feel a little . . . a little tense. Tempers are bound to. . ."

At this point Gribley forgot the rest of his sentence and stared over Fintan's shoulder at an unexpected sight. There were two terrifying-looking wild-haired figures charging up behind him with their teeth bared and their arms flailing. Mute with shock, he pointed weakly in their direction. Fintan turned around just in time to be knocked flat on his back by the shorter, fatter one of the wild people. He hit the ground heavily and had all the wind knocked out of him. The other assailant, who appeared to be a bony old woman with foul teeth and broken glasses, stopped running and brandished a big stick. Gribley stepped back, partly in fright and partly revolted by the appalling smell wafting from their ragged attackers. They smelled like a dustbin full of rotten meat which had been left in the sun all day . . . and garnished with goat's poo. He wasn't sure whether to feel terrified or just sick.

"I got him, Mum! Look! I finally got him!" hollered the fat man, pinning Fintan to the ground.

He seemed ecstatically pleased with himself. "I got him! I got him!"

The woman with the stick bared her horrible brown teeth and cackled with delight. "Yes!" she shrieked triumphantly. "He's ours at last!"

"What are you doing?" stammered Fintan beneath the foul-smelling, sweaty lump that was holding him down. "Get off me, will you! You smell terrible!"

"Yeah? Well you don't smell so great yerself, boy!" sniggered Eric, enjoying his moment of victory.

Gribley stepped forward and tried to intervene, but was walloped round the shoulder by Edith's stick.

"Stay back, you!" she yelled. "This is nothing to do with you. It's HIM we want!"

"Yeah!" added Eric, right into Fintan's face. "And we got him too! I've been looking forward to this moment for so long! You'll not be givin' us any more trouble now, will you, Fedora?"

Fintan, who was already hopelessly confused by this sudden turn of events, and happily oblivious to the entire kidnap plot, was taken aback. "What are you talking about?" he said, trying to avoid the man's appallingly bad breath. "How do you know my name? I've never seen you before in my life!"

This wasn't entirely true, but then again the Bumsteads were a lot scruffier now than when he'd briefly glimpsed them back at the airport.

"Oh yeah?" said Edith. "Don't come the innocent with us, boy! We've had more than enough of you and your tricks! But you're ours now, and so's your rich old daddy's money! You're well and truly kidnapped!"

"I beg your pardon?" said Gribley, thinking these unpleasant idiots must be suffering from the advanced stages of heatstroke. "Did you just say kidnapped?"

"You heard correct, Mister Clever Clogs!" grinned Edith. "And we came all the way from England for this!"

Gribley found this a little hard to believe. "Really? But why would you do that?" he asked, genuinely confused. "I don't understand. Why on earth would you come all the way to Brazil to kidnap him? Wouldn't it have made more sense to kidnap him in England? That's where he lives."

"That's enough of your lip, Mister Toffee Nose!" sneered Edith, swiping at him with her stick again but missing.

Gribley continued anyway. "Seriously, though," he said, "I'm intrigued. How are you intending to send his family the ransom demand? Have you got a satellite phone? Is there a postbox in the rainforest somewhere? Or are you planning on carrying him through the jungle and all the way back to England?"

Gradually Eric's victorious grin began to falter, as did his furious grip on Fintan's shoulders.

"Shut up!" he yelled without actually looking up. "Shut up, will you!"

To Edith's amazement, her large, lumpy son suddenly let go of their highly valuable prisoner and allowed him to scramble over to the safety of his butler. She was stunned.

"What are you doing?" she shouted. "What did you let him go for, you idiot? He'll get away!"

"Yeah? Well, so what if he does, Mother? What's the point, anyway?" wailed Eric, who was now kneeling dejectedly on the muddy riverbank. "The posh bloke's right, isn't he! What are we supposed to do with him, eh? We're not kidnappers! We're rubbish! We're failures!"

It had taken several days to happen, but it seemed Eric was finally coming to what remained of his senses. They'd been fooling themselves. It was all pointless. He slumped even further down into the mud and burst into a sudden flood of tears.

"Stop that, Eric!" hollered his unsympathetic mother. "Get up! Get up this minute, you useless lump!"

Fintan and Gribley took advantage of this development to take a few more paces backwards, towards some fresher air. Bemused, they stood and watched the bizarre spectacle of the scraggy old woman with the broken glasses screeching and ineptly whacking her son with her stick. It appeared he had no intention of getting up, but just sat there looking utterly broken and bawled his heart out. Whatever it was that had happened to these people for them to end up in such a state, Fintan couldn't imagine, but it must have been pretty extreme!

It was at this already slightly strange moment that a massive orange and white helicopter roared close overhead. Astonished, Gribley took off his big jungle hat and waved it furiously. Fintan followed suit. Eric, however, continued crying, and Edith continued hitting him.

Inside the police rescue helicopter, which had been following the course of the river, one of the crew caught a glimpse of what looked like a group of figures on the ground. There weren't quite as many as they'd expected to find and they were in the wrong place, but he was sure he'd seen something. He left his post and urgently alerted the pilot. A brief discussion followed with the navigator, who said they hadn't yet reached the coordinates they'd been given, so he must be mistaken. The spotter, however, insisted he'd definitely seen people down there and managed to persuade the pilot to circle back round and double-check. Sure enough, standing in the small muddy clearing by the merging rivers was a handful of people. The whole crew saw them this time.

Two of the figures on the ground were madly waving their hats to get their attention while a third had keeled over on his side, apparently injured, and was being assisted by a fourth. This must be them!

The pilot brought the helicopter as low as he could over the clearing and hovered above them. The door in its side slid open and a rescue line with a leather harness was winched down.

Fintan looked at Gribley and broke into a massive grin.

"Brilliant!" he shouted, over the noise of the helicopter. "Now that's what I call a real stroke of luck!"

Two helmeted crew men in dark green jumpsuits descended next and began organizing the rescue operation. One went over to assist the poor "injured" man lying on the ground while the other tried to establish that they'd found the right people.

"You Gonzalez?" he hollered to Gribley, who couldn't hear a thing he was saying over the noise of the helicopter.

"Pardon?" he shouted back, cupping a hand to his ear.

"Gonzalez? You Gonzalez, yes?" he repeated.

Fintan couldn't hear him either but gave his rescuer a big smile and a double thumbs up anyway. The man turned his attention to Fintan.

"You Wrench?" he said hopefully.

"I'm what?" said Fintan, thoroughly confused. "I'm winch?"

Suddenly the proverbial penny dropped. "Oh! I see what you mean!" he went on, nodding vigorously. "You want to winch us up! Winch! OK! Comprendo!"

This seemed to satisfy some of the man's doubts. "Where are others, please?" he yelled, looking around for the missing eighteen people.

"Others? What others?" said Fintan, turning to a still-deafened Gribley for help and not getting any.

"Twenty-two people," continued the rescuer, holding up his fingers several times to aid communication.

"Twenty-two?" That obviously wasn't right. Fintan thought he'd better put the poor confused foreign man straight.

"No, no, not twenty-two! Just two, see. Me and Gribs!" he shouted, pointing helpfully between Gribley and himself. "Oh, and there're those people over there, I suppose," he added as an afterthought, pointing towards Eric and Edith, who were having an equally pointless conversation with the paramedic. "We don't actually know them. They're kidnappers, you see. And they smell a bit." He held his nose and pulled a face to demonstrate the fact.

The man looked puzzled. "Kidnappers?" he said.

"Yeah! You know, kidnappers! Er ... baddies! Criminals!"

Despite the deafening noise from the helicopter overhead and the serious language barrier, this word seemed to translate perfectly well. "Criminals?" he repeated, suddenly looking very interested.

Fintan nodded again and made an unpleasant face indicating how much he didn't trust them. This news seemed to change the dynamics of the situation completely. The man strode directly over to his paramedic companion, took a good, hard look at the foul-smelling wild people, then yelled something urgent. Together they stepped back and began speaking into the little microphones in their helmets. Messages were exchanged with the rest of the helicopter crew, causing two more men, equipped with large scary-looking guns, to descend hurriedly to the ground. It was all getting really exciting! Fintan, who only a few minutes before had been feeling horribly despondent, was now having a fabulous time! It was like being in a movie!

Without hesitation the two armed policemen levelled their guns at the Bumsteads and shouted warnings in Portuguese. Edith dropped her stick, abandoned her son and attempted to make a run for it. She'd only hobbled a few steps when she was grabbed, pushed to the ground and handcuffed. As was Eric, who was feeling far too miserable to put up any resistance (other than the smell, of course, which had been causing the men a little hesitation). By this point, Fintan was so excited he'd even managed to forget how hungry he was! With the fugitives safely restrained, all four of the men turned to Fintan and Gribley, warmly shook them by the hand and congratulated them on their brilliant work.

"It was nothing!" said Fintan with complete honesty, while somehow managing to sound fabulously modest.

Having donned their rucksacks, the brave crime-fighting heroes were helped into the harness and lifted into the waiting helicopter, where the other crew members also offered their congratulations. The navigator pointed happily to a **Police Wanted** poster stuck to the inside of the open hatchway. It seemed an odd coincidence, but it was a photo-fit picture of the smelly pair being restrained below. Fintan and Gribley exchanged smiles of relief, tinged with a tiny bit of pride. Not only had they just been rescued from a terrible fate but had apparently captured Brazil's most wanted criminals too! The day wasn't turning out so badly after all!

Gonzalez's day, on the other hand, had ended up being a big disappointment. Several hours had passed and there was still no sign of the rescue helicopter. He wondered where it could have got to. The men were getting restless, hungry and thirsty, and had started arguing with each other. Scuffles broke out when someone found half a burnt meat pie that had survived the exploding hut. Max Wrench, meanwhile, was hopelessly delirious. All day long he wandered around annoying the men by asking them if they had seen Barbara. Several times they had to restrain him to stop him wandering off into the forest in search of his hotel. Gonzalez tried calling for help again and again but got no answer. By the time darkness fell, everyone was in a foul mood.

Eventually, the following afternoon, after many attempts and much swearing, he got a signal on the satellite phone. The emergency services, however, were confused.

"What?" said the woman on the end of the line. "But we rescued you yesterday! Are you lost again already?"

Gonzalez was stunned. "No you didn't!" he yelled. "We're still sitting here waiting for you!"

"Well, not according to my records, you aren't!" continued the woman, consulting a written report on her desk.

It was at this point that Gonzalez completely lost his temper and said a few unwise and unhelpful things. She hung up. It took another call and nearly half an hour of apologies before the emergency services agreed to send out another rescue helicopter.

"Has anyone seen Barbara?" said Wrench to a tree, and wandered off into the forest again.

THIRTY

Despite the cold, the drizzle and the grey skies, Fintan was happy to be back in England. It had been a long, tiring return journey, but at least he and Gribley had been spared the ocean crossing this time and taken a plane. Since his brilliant helicopter ride, Fintan had been cured of his fear of flying and was now something of a convert to the joys of air travel. Which was lucky, as all the Atlantic cruise line companies had refused to let him on board. The only problem now was that the big black car they'd borrowed was still parked at the Southampton docks, many miles away from the airport they arrived at. Consequently, one train and two buses later, Fintan and Gribley found themselves sitting in the back of a taxi contentedly watching the scenery pass by. After all the danger and excitement of the past couple of weeks, everything seemed wonderfully normal.

The taxi pulled into the driveway of Fedora Hall and dropped them right outside the house. They were just hauling their battered, mud-caked luggage out of the boot when Fintan's father appeared at the front door.

"Ah! So the wanderers return, eh!" he said, smiling through his huge moustache. "All's well, I hope?"

"Hello, Dad!" said Fintan, not sure whether he should shake his hand or hug him. He awkwardly tried a bit of both. "All fine, thanks! Glad to be home."

Sir Filbert shook Gribley's hand and thanked him for escorting his "difficult" youngest son, which was a job well beyond the call of normal duty.

"Behaved himself, did he? The boy?" he asked.

"Most of the time, sir, yes," said Gribley diplomatically.

Between them, they gathered up the pile of rucksacks and dirty boots and carried them into the hall. Flavian and Felicity, the annoying elder siblings, appeared and immediately resumed their favourite sport of Fintan-baiting. "Good grief!" said Felicity. "Little brother's back! Thought we'd seen the last of you!"

"Crikey, so he is!" added Flavian in mock amazement. "Been camping in the front garden all this time, have we?"

The pair of them then high-fived each other and snorted with laughter. They seemed to find this hilarious.

"Oh, ha ha!" scowled Fintan, who was then smothered by the sudden arrival of his mother.

"Ooh, look! It's my brave little explorer!" she cooed, giving him a big wet kiss on the cheek. "Home all safe and sound! I've been ever so worried!"

"Mum!" he protested. "I'm not little!"

His irritating siblings found this highly amusing too.

Any detailed reporting of his epic adventure, however, had to wait until Fintan had washed his hands and his mother had spread a few sheets of newspaper on the sofa for him to sit on.

"So!" began Mr Filbert, clapping his hands

together expectantly as the whole family gathered in the drawing room. "How was the big trek?"

Gribley gestured for Fintan to be the bearer of the good news.

"Well," he said, "it was brilliant, actually! A complete success!"

"What?" said Felicity. "You mean you didn't get lost as soon as you got outside the gates? I don't believe it!"

"There's always a first time for everything!" added Flavian, guffawing at his own wit.

"Now then, you two!" chastised their mother. "Let your little brother tell his story!"

Fintan frowned. It seemed nothing at all had changed. No one had taken him seriously before the expedition, and they weren't taking him any more seriously now. He decided to skip all the exciting details, the tales of hardship, pain, suffering, amazing discoveries and even more amazing coincidences and cut straight to the grand unveiling of his treasure.

"All right, then. . ." he announced defiantly. "Take a look at this!"

He unzipped his dirty rucksack, which his

mother had insisted be placed on several sheets of newspaper to protect the carpet, and pulled out a small plastic box. The family looked intrigued and leaned forward in their seats to see what he'd brought back. Biting his lip in anticipation, Fintan proudly peeled off the airtight lid, lifted out a crumpled paper parcel and carefully placed it on the coffee table.

"Ooh!" said his mother. "What is it? It's nothing nasty, is it?"

"This, Mother," announced Fintan dramatically, "is the rarest, most precious and most delicious fruit in the entire world!"

With great ceremony, using only his fingertips, he gently unwrapped the parcel.

"Prepare yourselves for nothing less than the legendary great Brazilian choco—"

He froze in mid-sentence. Plonked in the middle of the family coffee table, on a page torn from *Young Adventurer* magazine, were the sad remains of a stale peanut butter sandwich cut into neat little squares.

"Bit funny-looking, isn't it?" said his father, peering at it in faint disgust.

Fintan turned to Gribley and gaped in horror.

"Where's it gone?" he squeaked, losing all control over his voice. "Where's it gone, Gribs! What's happened?"

Flavian and Felicity instigated a sarcastic round of applause and made more unfunny remarks which Fintan didn't hear. His mind was elsewhere.

"You know what this means, don't you?" he muttered to Gribley, as all the colour drained from his face. "I ate it, didn't I! I didn't eat the sandwich . . . I ate the chocoplum!"

"It would certainly appear so, sir," said Gribley sympathetically. "Most unfortunate. However, not to worry. I fortunately took the precaution of bringing along a spare one, in case of accidents."

As Fintan sat white-faced and open-mouthed, gaping like a very ill fish, Gribley produced a small, carefully wrapped container from his bag and handed it over. "You can show them this one instead if you like, sir."

Sir Filbert was especially impressed. This thing wasn't even supposed to exist outside of legend and daft boys' adventure stories, and yet there it was in real life. Reddish brown and beautifully shiny and sitting on his coffee table!

"Well, I never! The Brazilian chocoplum! Who'd have thought it!" he said, coming closer for a better look. "Well done, young man! I honestly didn't think you had it in you!"

This was the closest thing to a compliment Fintan could ever remember hearing from his father.

"Well, Gribley did a lot of the work!" he said, but glowed with pride anyway.

"Are you sure you're allowed to bring it into the country?" said Flavian, who was desperately trying to think of something to find fault with. "Weren't you supposed to declare it at customs?"

Fintan shrugged and paid no attention.

"So you only got the one then, did you? Is that all you could manage?" added Felicity sarcastically, and received a very stern look from her mother. Fintan ignored them both. He wasn't going to let his obnoxious brother and sister spoil this moment.

"Any idea what it tastes like?" asked Sir Filbert, slowly coming to terms with the chocoplum's potentially huge commercial value.

"Not really," said Fintan, and exchanged a guilty

glance with Gribley. It was true, though. The only memory he had of his sleep-eating incident was that he had woken up feeling very full and very happy. "We'll have to give it a try!"

Gribley was dispatched to the kitchen and returned with china plates, tiny silver forks, a very sharp knife and with the chocoplum centred on a large platter. With great care and precision, he carved the fruit into thin slices and distributed them among the family. Beneath the fuzzy brown skin lay a beautiful pale-yellow pulp and a single smooth, black stone. The taste was extraordinary. A fabulous mixture of the warm creaminess of chocolate and the sweet juiciness of a plum, yet not really quite like either. A completely new and unique flavour.

Everyone was unbelievably impressed. Even Felicity and Flavian found themselves being complimentary! If they could grow this fruit in their greenhouse, it would mean a secure future for Fedora Fancies. Possibly even a fortune in extra sales! Fintan was suddenly looking like a vital member of the beloved family business!

THIRTY-ONE

Three weeks passed. Back in Brazil, a seriously traumatized Gonzalez had decided to take an early retirement. His recent unpleasant encounters with fire, water, piranhas, biting ants, exploding helicopters and dog wee had been enough to put him off the business world for good. In search of a far simpler life, he had moved into a small, isolated hut with no electricity or flushing toilets. There he spent his days tending his meagre vegetable garden and trying to stop his hands trembling. Every day he counted his blessings that he never had to see Fintan Fedora again! He may have been utterly penniless, but at least he was safe!

Meanwhile, the Brazilian authorities had wasted no time in finding Eric and Edith Bumstead guilty of a long string of offences and locked them away. Despite daily hot showers to ensure they didn't upset their fellow prisoners, there were soon enough complaints about the revolting pair to have them removed. A brief court hearing deported them back to England, where they were split up and put in separate prisons. Edith found herself sharing a cell with some women who were, unbelievably, even nastier than she was. This, at least, gave her plenty to moan about. Eric, meanwhile, had sunk even deeper into despondency. All his dreams of gold-plated taps in the shape of swans had come to nothing. All he had now was a mouldy, lukewarm shower which he had to share with several other horrible hairy inmates. His life was nothing but boredom and misery. To make things even worse, he had ended up in the same prison as his long-lost father, "Nosher" Bumstead, the notorious armed robber, who had read all about his son's exploits in the newspapers. He wasn't proud. Having a fat, useless failed kidnapper as a son was ruining his reputation! It wasn't a happy family reunion.

A different sort of reputation had also been ruined at Giganti-Foods International. Randall's handling of the Brazilian business had cost the company a fortune. Sales of their cake products had plummeted and many jobs had been lost. Not Randall's, because he was the boss and got to decide whose jobs disappeared. This, of course, made him even less popular. His name had become a joke in the food business. He was the idiot who made a multimillion-dollar fuss about something that he didn't have, and probably didn't even exist. Even in his own office building, people sniggered as he passed in the corridors and whispered things like "There goes the chocoplum king!"

As a result of all this, Randall had taken to spending long periods of the day locked in the toilet, whimpering. The only thing that gave him any consolation at all was the knowledge that no one else had the chocoplums either! That would have finished him off for good!

There had also been big changes in the world of Max Wrench. He was a changed man. The vicious, ruthless businessman had disappeared and been replaced by a softer, more timid, more understanding man. This new Wrench, now that he was unemployed and freed from the corrupting world of big business, enjoyed nothing more than helping his wife, Barbara, around the house. His days revolved around cleaning, washing up, walking the poodle and listening to her irritating voice telling him what a loser he was. Occasionally, in the middle of the night, he would have little flashes of memory involving a strange annoying boy. For some reason these flashbacks left him wide awake, sweaty and twitching. Other than that he remembered nothing, and had miraculously become almost pleasant! Perhaps there was something therapeutic about being hit over the head with a heavy iron cooking pot.

Meanwhile, back at Fedora Hall, Gribley's life had very quickly returned to normal. Back to good old basic domestic duties. His days were all very much the same: dull, predictable and hard work, which, oddly enough, was exactly how he liked it. Being employed to look after Fintan always seemed to swing wildly between long periods of safe, boring familiarity and shorter phases of wild, dangerous madness. Not that he wasn't secretly fond of a little excitement, but on the whole he much preferred the boring bits.

Every evening after finishing the ironing, he would reward himself with a long, leisurely soak in the bath, reading a good book. There he lay, perfectly content and happy with his lot in life. On the soap tray in front of him he had arranged a hot cup of tea in a china cup and two triangular slices of buttered toast with the finest English honey. Luxury.

Until there was a little knock on the bathroom door.

"Gribs? Are you in there?" called Fintan's voice from the landing. Gribley made a vague noise, which sort of acknowledged he was there but would ideally rather be left in peace.

"It's me!" said Fintan, accidentally bumping into a vase and sending it crashing to the floor, just in case there might be some doubt.

It would be nice to report that Fintan had returned from the rainforest older, wiser, and less of a disaster, but this wouldn't be entirely true. Admittedly he was three weeks older, but there was still no sign of any wisdom and little evidence of him growing out of his unfortunate clumsiness. On the plus side, though, his father now took him a little more seriously, and was even wavering on his decision to ban him from the family business. Felicity and Flavian were incredibly annoyed at this prospect. They even found themselves grudgingly accepting that their little brother had achieved something pretty important. Especially since there had been little signs of life in the greenhouse.

"I've got some good news!" continued Fintan. "Well, two bits of good news, actually! Mum just told me the chocoplum tree has sprouted! She says it looks really, really healthy and is growing fast! Brilliant, eh?"

This was great news. Fintan had been feeling extremely guilty for what had happened in the jungle. He had already written half a dozen letters of apology to Correntina and Ana, sent them some money for a new boat and was now looking forward to being able to send them cuttings of the plant too. Hopefully it could be arranged that the grove was replanted one day, only this time he wouldn't be telling anyone! Especially not ambitious employees of Giganti-Foods International!

"That is indeed excellent news, sir. Many congratulations," said Gribley, hoping to be left to his tea and his reading. "I look forward to seeing it soon."

"Yeah! Can't wait till it starts growing some little baby chocoplums!" added Fintan from the other side of the closed door. "Oh, and one other thing! I hope you've got some warm clothes in your wardrobe, Gribs, cos I've just been reading a brilliant new article in *Young Adventurer* magazine! It's all about these totally rare fruits called Icelandic snowberries!"

Gribley slid further into his bathwater so that it covered his ears, and draped a warm flannel over his eyes. He just wanted to make the safe, boring phase last a tiny bit longer.

Clive Goddard has been on plenty of disastrous adventures. He was once stranded in the USA by a volcanic eruption, has been chased by an angry ostrich in Swaziland, and had his rucksack soaked by a leaky toilet in Holland. He got sunburn in Hawaii, heatstroke in Namibia, a poisonous spider bite in South Africa and food poisoning in Thailand. He lost his camera in Tasmania, lost himself in Japan and got robbed in China (twice).

Clive Goddard didn't know he was a writer until this book happened. He thought he was a cartoonist. It was probably illustrating a dozen or so *Horribly Famous* books that gave him this idea.

When not travelling, drawing or writing, Clive lives in Oxford where he rides a bike, plays badminton and practices sleeping for long periods of time.

READY FOR FINTAN'S NEXT ADVENTURE?

HERE'S A SNEAK PEEK...

ONE

The plane was descending rapidly through a dense layer of freezing cloud. Fintan pressed his nose against the window and tried to catch a glimpse of the bizarre, rugged landscape below. Iceland looked weird, multicoloured, and wrinkly.

"Look at that!" he said excitedly, grabbing Gribley by his coat sleeve. "It's like some strange alien planet!"

Gribley didn't really want to look. In fact he didn't really want to be there at all.

"No thank you, sir," he said, far more interested in reading his book.

Fintan didn't mind. He knew the expedition was going to be utterly brilliant and he was excited enough for both of them. They were on a quest to discover the mysterious and fabulously rare Icelandic Snowberry. A virtually unknown fruit which, according to *Young Adventurer* magazine, was rumoured only to grow thousands of feet up on the misty slopes of extinct volcanoes. If Fintan was lucky enough to find a living specimen he was going to bring it back to England and make a fortune! He would be known as "Fintan Fedora, the Intrepid Explorer and Discoverer of the Legendary Icelandic Snowberry". It was going to be a difficult and dangerous quest that would take him up mountains and across glaciers, through snow and ice and fire; a journey across strange landscapes of boiling mud and violently hot geysers. He was about as excited as it was possible for a human being to get without actually bursting.

Which explains why he was so disappointed when they got off the plane; the airport souvenir shop was stocked with hundreds of jars of snowberry jam.

TWO

"Morning, loser!" shouted an arrogant voice from the hallway. "Want some toast with snowberry jam for breakfast?"

"*Snow* good talking to him," added another voice, falling apart with mocking laughter. "He's *berry* stupid!"

It was Fintan's horrible older brother and sister, Flavian and Felicity, whose favourite hobby was making fun of him. He had been back home at Fedora Hall for nearly a week now and they were still teasing him about the disastrous Icelandic trip. It looked like it wasn't going to be forgotten in a hurry. The sooner Fintan could get out of the house on another adventure the better.

He did his best to ignore them and made his way

to the kitchen, where Gribley was seated at the table reading a small blue book.

"Morning, Gribs," he said brightly. "Has the postman been yet?"

"He has indeed, sir," announced Gribley, marking his place in the book and getting up from the table.

Fintan rubbed his hands gleefully, knocking over a box of cereal with his elbow. "Brilliant!" he said. "It's *Young Adventurer* magazine day at last!"

Gribley fetched the post and started making the breakfast. He could have let Fintan make his own of course but that often led to one of the boy's little accidents. And it was far too nice a morning to be spoilt by the sound of broken plates and smoke alarms going off. There were still black soot stains under the kitchen cupboards from the time Fintan had set fire to the toaster, and a hole in the worktop where he had melted the kettle.

"Thanks, Gribs," said Fintan as he was presented with a mug of sweet tea and a pile of toast buried in peanut butter.

Things didn't get much better than this. A good breakfast, a sunny day with no school and a whole new magazine to read! All he needed now was for

Flavian and Felicity to be abducted by aliens to make the day perfect. He tore the plastic wrapping from the latest *Young Adventurer* and surveyed the cover. It was an exciting drawing of a fishing boat crew grappling with a giant squid, hacking at its tentacles with axes. Fintan thought it was brilliant!

The rest of the magazine was just as good: an exciting mix of amazing "facts" from around the world and action-packed adventure stories; fabulous stuff about man-eating tigers, mysterious snake-charmers and rumbling volcanoes. There was an excellent article on dog sleds falling into deep crevasses in the Antarctic, and photos of exotic islands where the crabs climbed trees and the local tribes hadn't changed since the Stone Age. There were fantastic colour drawings of extinct giant sloths and armoured pangolins the size of buses. He settled down to read a story about an expedition that headed into the forests of New Guinea and were never seen again. Headhunters were suspected to have eaten them!

"Don't forget to eat your breakfast, sir," reminded Gribley, sitting down again with his little blue book.

"Oh right," said Fintan.

He took a huge mouthful of cold toast. "What's that you're reading, Gribs?"

Gribley was surprised the boy had even noticed he was in the room, let alone that he was holding a book!

"It's a volume of ancient Chinese poetry, sir. *The Song of the Moon Dragon*."

"Oh," said Fintan, immediately losing interest. He didn't like poetry.

"It was written eight hundred years ago by the Great Master of Yin," added Gribley.

Fintan nodded but couldn't think of anything else to say. He knew absolutely nothing about ancient Chinese poetry and was quite happy for it to stay that way. He gulped down some lukewarm tea and returned to a story about two-headed white bats living deep in the caves of Patagonia.

"It is the poet's great unfinished masterpiece, sir," continued Gribley.

"What is?" said Fintan, wondering whether two-headed bats ever bit themselves by mistake.

Gribley sighed. "*The Song of the Moon Dragon*, sir. The book of Chinese poetry which I mentioned a few seconds ago."

"Oh right," said Fintan. "Unfinished. A bit boring then, is it?"

Gribley winced. Sometimes talking to Fintan was like trying to explain ballet dancing to a dog.

"Not at all, sir, it's actually very interesting. The Great Master of Yin was a multi-talented man. As well as being a poet he was also an artist and a sculptor. The great tragedy is that he disappeared before he could finish his finest work. In fact his whole village disappeared. According to legend the village of Yin was a fabulously beautiful place with towering gold pagodas filled with many of the Great Master's treasures. Including the legendary Moon Dragon, itself carved in gold . . . and no one has ever found it."

"Cool," said Fintan, half listening and half looking at a drawing of Bigfoot, who was ten feet tall with shaggy white fur and massive scary teeth.

In the centre pages of the magazine he found an illustrated article about the Great Wall of China.

"Hey, look at this, Gribs," he said. "There's a thing about China in here! Apparently there's a really big old wall there."

Gribley looked up. "Indeed, sir," he said. "The

famous Great Wall of China. I believe it is over six thousand kilometres long."

"Wow," said Fintan, impressed with Gribley's ability to remember astonishing facts. "That must have taken a lot of bricks! Is it anywhere near the place you were talking about?"

Gribley was surprised the boy had even been listening.

"The lost village of Yin, sir?" he said. "I'm afraid Yin has been lost for eight hundred years. No one is even sure where it was to begin with."

"Lost for eight hundred years, eh?" mused Fintan.

Gribley held his breath. There was a look on the boy's face which suggested he was getting one of his dangerous ideas. The sort of idea which usually led to poor old Gribley being dragged away from home on some terrible expedition.

"Well in that case. . ." announced Fintan, closing his magazine, "it's about time someone found it!"